Who Would've Thought?

RAVEN SMITH

ISBN: 978-1-953181-08-4 (Paperback)

This novel is a work of fiction. Any references to real people, events, establishments, or locations are intended only to give the story a sense of reality and authenticity. Other names and incidents occurring in the work are either the product of the author's imagination. Any character that happens to share the same of a person who is an acquaintance of the author, past or present, is present is purely coincidental and is in no way intended to be an actual account involving that person or people.

Printed in the United States of America.

First printing, 2021.

Happie Face Publishing Company

DEDICATION

Dedicated to Nakeem A. Coleman.

CONTENTS

Who Would've Thought?   1

Facing the Truth   6

Lessons From a Single Man   12

Don't Overthink   19

She's Mine   23

Hennessy and a Question   28

Nothing But Business   32

Under His Control   53

Snakes Are Not Your Friend   62

Trying to Understand   70

Being Exposed   78

Situationships   89

Accepting Change   97

Listen to Me   106

Backstabbing Me   114

Needing Help   129

Over and Done   139

Give and Take   147

Coming to an End   154

About RAVEN SMITH   161

WHO WOULD'VE THOUGHT?
Adrian

"So, let me get this correct before we go any further. You're stating that you are planning on getting a divorce because you walked in on your wife having sex with another woman?" I was kind of baffled.

Looking at Chris, all I wanted to do was smack him to make him realize that's every man's fantasy.

"Exactly! That's exactly what I'm telling you, man. I couldn't believe it myself," Christopher told me while lying on the couch in my bachelor pad.

Christopher was my childhood friend and my college roommate, so I knew this man more than I knew myself at some points. I couldn't believe it when he got married five years ago. We were supposed to be Batman and Robin in the streets, but he got hit with the love bug. I was happy for him... I just thought it was a big mistake at the time. I admit, I was biased back then; I mean who enjoys seeing their wingman go?

"So, explain to me how having two naked women in your bed is a

1

bad situation to have? The Chris I once knew would have loved that idea."

"It's not just a woman, it's my wife," he states like that explains it.

I threw my hands up in the air. "Wow! Really? So, is she not your wife anymore?" I asked sarcastically.

I know that I'm not married or trying to settle down any time soon, but if this is what married life is about–nothing but confusion–y'all can keep it. I can see how strangely heartbroken Chris is right now, but I'm just trying to help him find the silver lining in all of this.

"Come on man you're not helping the situation here. This is serious. I really don't know what to do here."

"Well for one, sit up on the couch. You're lying there like you're depressed." Chris sat up with a sad look on his face.

"I'm not depressed. I'm hurt, confused and lost."

"I'm not done–two look at like this. At least it's another vagina and not a penis. Did you even ask or talk to Renee about what you saw?"

Chris sat up even more and it's evident on his face he's hurt by the whole ordeal. "No, I came straight over here," he told me.

I got up and head to the kitchen. "You want a drink?" I asked, hoping to take his mind off things.

"Yeah, you got any Henny, E&J, or Crown Royal over there? Shoot, at this point, I'll take some tequila to erase this shit from my memory."

I looked at Chris with this bizarre look on my face. It shocked me that he wanted something that hard and wanted to forget what he saw. I grabbed a Snapple apple juice from the refrigerator.

"Man, you don't need all that. You need a clear mind space before you go back to your wife. So, take this Snapple and be happy. So, where were we, oh yeah, did you even recognize the other woman?"

"No, I don't know the other woman. I didn't have a chance to look at her. Her head was buried between my wife's legs. You're sure you don't have anything stronger than this?"

The image was hot to me, but I quickly had to remind myself that it was a sensitive subject.

"So how about this my friend, after this one drink–and I do mean one, because I don't need you to be drunk–you'll see Renee. You need to talk to your wife before you start thinking about a divorce." I stared at Chris as I took a shot of Henny and handed him a shot.

"You know I'm against marriage, but to each its own. I just still believe in loyalty and dedication and Renee had your back for far too long to count," I explained to him.

"But this is cheating. Infidelity, Adrian. How am I supposed to get past that?"

"Christopher, this is me you talking to. I remember you still running wild in the beginning of your marriage, or are you forgetting who was there right with you? You took that vow through all the madness for the rest of your life, so work through it. If you two can decide if it's unrepairable, then okay, do what you have to do. But as for me, you two will always sound better than one."

"What if that's what she wants now, Adrian? Like what if that's what she's attracted to?" He questioned me like I had the answers.

I leaned forward and spoke to him on his eye level.

"Let me tell you this about women. They will have eyes just like we do. They will find other women attractive. Some don't mind letting it be known. Some go as far as being in a relationship, some like to have company of another woman in the bedroom. One thing is for sure, a woman is and always will be a work of art. Something that's admired and cherished. When it comes to seduction, they have men beat by far. So many men have gone to war and died over these masterpieces. So, it's okay for them to appreciate the same as us. It's 2020, Chris. You'll be surprised though. I bet it had something to do with the lack of sex in the marriage. Watch." I told him as I grabbed my cell phone off the table, checking my notifications.

"For you to be single all the time, you sure make it seem like you have it all figured out when it to comes to women," Chris said slyly.

"No, it's not that. I just pay attention to details when it comes to women and keep it simple. The reason I'm always single is because I don't want to end up like you."

"That's a low blow, Ad, and you know it," Chris said while laying back down on the couch.

"It was and I'm sorry about that, but anyone knows me knows that I have commitment issues, and I'll admit that! I was raised by a bunch of women and they're no different than us men. They might even be worse," I said with a horrified expression. "Here's my logic. Women call men dogs because we just want to hump. You ever wonder why the term 'bitch' became applicable to them? A female dog in heat, putting her rump on display. I believe they only started getting offended when their secret got exposed. It has become offensive ever since then." I explained, walking over to him.

I reached my hand out. "Come on get up," I told him.

"Where are we going?" Chris asked standing to his feet.

"It's where you're going. I need you to snap out of it and go home to your wife. Be a man and be confident and talk to her about what you saw," I told him, pushing him towards the door as I open it.

"Make sure you call me later and tell me about it and if it goes bad for you and you need somewhere to go, please don't come here crying."

"Some best friend you are, Ad." Chris stated, stepping out the door.

"I'm always here for you, but I have an appointment tonight with someone special. I need to get ready for it, so bye-bye and good luck friend. Call me," I said while closing the door behind him.

FACING THE TRUTH
Christopher

Man, that damn Adrian. I couldn't believe him. I was in need, and instead of letting me crash at his place, he threw me into the fire by sending me back to the enemy. *Should I even go home*? Obviously, my wife didn't miss me. Damn, I couldn't believe she betrayed me like this.

But I had to go home–if not for myself, then at least for my princess. If she doesn't see me come into that house, she'll have a thousand questions for me. I wondered when kids get to be so smart. She was my pride and joy. I just wasn't ready to confront Renee, but once again I knew Adrian was right; I needed to talk to my wife.

I had no idea where the time went, but soon enough, I pulled into my driveway. I turned the engine and lights off and sat there preparing myself mentally. I dreaded this conversation because it was going to lead to confrontation that I wanted to avoid.

I took a breath, gathered myself, and open the car door thinking it was now or never. As the cool air hit me, I began to relax for a moment. I could see the lights on inside the house.

I took another deep breath and put the key in the door just before it swung open. Renee was standing there in her pajamas. I knew she must have been watching me the whole time.

"Hey," I greeted her as I walked past her to get into the house. "Smells good. What you cook?" I asked, taking a whiff of the aroma.

"Thanks, and just some ribs, baked macaroni and broccoli. I fixed your plate, it's in the microwave," Renee said, closing the door and following me into the kitchen.

I washed my hands before retrieving my plate from the microwave, placing it on the counter. It looked delicious and smelled even better, but then something hits me.

"Where's Siren?" I asked, grabbing a fork from the drawer and digging into my baked macaroni.

"She is at my mom's house," Renee said taking a seat on the other side of the island counter. "I didn't think she needed to be around for this."

"Around for what?" I ask while looking up from my plate.

"Come on Christopher, I know you saw me earlier. I heard the door shut behind you when you left," Renee said with her head down, avoiding eye contact. I was tempted to act naïve but decided not to play with her since she looked pitiful. She was normally a confident woman.

"When did you turn gay?"

"I'm not gay," she scoffed. I looked at her like she was crazy and dug back into my food. "I'm not Chris, you know me. I'm your wife."

"Sure, didn't seem like it earlier," I countered.

7

"I'm going to act like I didn't hear that, Christopher."

I snapped. "No, acknowledge it! I want you to because what type of nerve do you have to catch a damn attitude? I come home to my house, to be greeted by my wife, in our bed with her legs open with a woman's head where it doesn't belong!" I yelled, throwing my fork in the sink. She suddenly made me lose my appetite.

"Where are you going? We're talking Christopher!" she questioned, following me out the kitchen and upstairs into our bedroom. I just ignored her as I grabbed a bag and tossed it on the bed.

"You're not going nowhere!" She snatched the bag from off the bed and threw it across the room. "We're going to finish talking." She stood strong and tall in front of me despite her small frame with her arms out like that was going to stop me from.

"Okay, well let's talk then since that's what you want to do." I took a seat on the edge of the bed. "Come on, talk!"

"Baby, I know you're mad, but it's not what you think, Chris."

"So, let me think again. I guess that was... umm your OB/GYN doing a house call, huh?" I asked.

"Stop being smart and let's have a real conversation, Chris. I love you; I mean, you're the love of my life, but lately we just seem like friends rather than lovers. I was honestly trying to put some spice back into our love life."

I looked at her and all I could see was another bitch in between her legs. I didn't know who this person is anymore. How could she say it puts spice back in our love life? What, I wasn't good enough for her? Like, you'd rather have another pussy than dick? Free dick, your husband dick. Make it make sense.

"Don't you think I know what time you get off by now. I wanted to try something different for us. But instead, I looked like a fool," Renee confessed leaning against the dresser.

I took in what she said and dwelled on it for a moment. *Am I tripping for taking this hard?* I asked myself. This all could've been fixed if she just waited for me to get home. I would've loved a threesome, but that shit was over.

"I don't want you to hate me. I made a mistake, but it wasn't for some selfish pleasure," she pleaded as tears freely flowed down her face.

I couldn't say anything to her because everything she said pissed me off. How could she say it wasn't for selfish pleasure when a bitch that I didn't even know was eating her out like a grown ass man?

Before I knew it, I was getting mad all over again. I wanted to stand firm, but my love for her made me console her. I couldn't take her breaking down. She was still my wife.

"It's alright Renee. I still love you."

"So, you're not leaving me?" she asked, sniffling and crying.

"I can't answer that right now. I'm still hurt, but I'm here now," I said, and she squeezed me even harder as she pulled me closer to her.

"Please don't tell nobody about this," she said as she wiped the tears out of her eyes. I could tell her intention was good, but her execution was terrible.

"It's too late for that. Adrian already knows," I informed her.

"OH MY GOD!" Renee groaned putting her head in my chest.

"Listen, I need you to be honest with me. Can you do that?" I asked, stepping back to look at her in her eyes. I could tell she was reading my mind already and knew what I was about to ask her.

"I can do that," she told me.

"Are you into women?"

I couldn't believe I was asking my wife if she was gay.

"I am not gay, Christopher. I told you where my state of mind was at."

"Did you enjoy it?" I asked with my eyes penetrating hers.

"What type of question is that? I'm not answering that," she said, turning away from me and that's all the confirmation I needed.

"Have it your way."

"What does that mean?" she asked.

"Nothing. Excuse me; I need to take a shower," I said, heading towards the bathroom. I needed time to think to myself and that's exactly what I got when I closed the bathroom door.

Looking into the mirror, I questioned myself. I didn't know what to believe. Was I still man enough for my wife? I tried being the good guy. I went to work and came home and took care of my family. I might still dabble in my old activities, but I was wise enough to know when enough was enough.

If she wanted to take that for granted, fine. If it's spice that she wanted, then it's spice she was going to get. I'm done being a faithful husband. If that's what she wants, then let's have some fun. She probably was cheating and just got caught.

I finished my shower, grabbed a few sheets, and headed downstairs to the couch. I didn't want to share that bed with her tonight.

I wanted payback.

LESSONS FROM A SINGLE MAN
Adrian

My phone went off. It was a text message from Dominic asking me, where I was. For real, I just wanted to stay home. I had a long day with an annoying ass client. I really didn't feel like dealing with people, but I decided to go out because I'm a good friend.

I replied with, where are we going? If he doesn't respond in the next five min—*Ding!* I heard my phone go off. *Please don't be him, please don't…. Shit.*

I was supposed to be meeting my friends at this nice place called OOKA for a couple of drinks and a bite to eat. Plus, I knew my man Chris could use the time away from Renee, and I felt kind of bad for pushing him out the door like I did.

So, inviting my two friends from college made it a men's night out altogether. I was actually running late, so I told Dominic that my last meeting lasted longer than I expected. Being a real estate agent in Pennsylvania wasn't an easy career, but it sure was a profitable one, and I was happy in the line of work.

Finding a parking spot at the restaurant turned out to be more of a challenge than I thought. I wasn't expecting the place to be crowded, but I should have known it would be on a Friday night.

I found a spot, quickly texted the fellas, letting them know I was there. Then I made sure I had everything I needed and headed out toward the restaurant.

The atmosphere of OOKA was a sophisticated one. With its white and black decor, it always gave me that grown and sexy vibe.

"Good evening, sir and welcome to OOKA. My name is Sarah and I'll be your hostess for the evening. Is it just you?"

"Actually, I have reservations with a group of friends of mine. I believe it's under Collins, Christopher Collins," I stated as she looked over her reservation list.

"Yes, I see. Sorry right this way," she said as she led me to the table where the fellas were sitting. As I walked through the restaurant, I couldn't help but to check her out. She just didn't seem like my type, but I definitely enjoyed the view of her walk.

"It's about time you showed up. What took you so long?" Jake asked as soon as I reached the table.

"Nothing man, I just had this annoying client that didn't understand the word 'tomorrow.'" I told the group while trying to sit in my chair. "I was trying to close a deal with a client of mine."

"Some people are just stubborn in this world."

"I hear that," Christopher and Dominic say in unison.

"So, what have I missed so far?" I asked, rubbing my hands together as I order a drink.

"Nothing really, just catching up on life and for the last few minutes and making eye contact with the group of women seated at that table over there." Dominic informed me while also pointing to the table the women were seated at.

They were behind me, so I had to turn around. They were three equally beautiful women in their own way. The left looked bossy, the middle was the quiet one, and the right was the goofy one. All I could see was a challenge.

"So why are you guys still over here?" I asked, not understanding the problem.

"I'm married, I don't have nothing to do with this," Chris said, flashing his ring on his finger and taking a sip from his cup.

"So, what's y'all's excuse?" I asked Jake and Dominic, who just shrugged their shoulders. I thought to myself that my friends are pathetic. If Chris wasn't married, at least he would be up for the challenge.

"You know if you want something in life, you don't get it by staring at it. You have to be ready and willing to go get it. That includes women too, you know." I started while moving around the table to get a better view of the ladies. "You know women love confidence. And I mean confidence, not cockiness."

"So, you're telling us to go for it?" Jake asked.

"Exactly."

"We should send them some drinks or a bottle or something," Dominic suggested, to which Chris and Jake agree to.

"Does this look like a club?" I asked, thinking that these men cannot be my friends right now. We used to send girls drinks when we were boys, now we are men, we got to handle our business. "Do they look like fast women or classy women? Matter of fact, what kind are you looking for?"

"Come on, where are you going with this?" Christopher asked, getting a bit agitated by my line of questioning.

"I'm saying good thought, but the wrong scene for that type of gesture. Look at these women. They are mature."

"By that, you mean old." Jake quips.

"Jake, I'm trying to be decent here, but yes, they might be older. Look how they dress, classy and kind of conservative, but feminine. You ever notice when you first start buying a woman something or footing the bill, they start to expect that. I like to give a woman a chance to show she can handle her own."

"So, what do you suggest, love doctor?" Chris asked.

"Better yet, why don't you give us a demonstration," Dominic suggested.

I had no problem showing these guys how to get a girl. They needed the pointers and tips because they all needed help.

"Perfect idea, Dom. Come on love doctor, go show us how it's done correctly," Chris said, egging me on.

"Is that what y'all want?" I asked with a questionable expression.

"I think it will be a good learning experience."

I took a long, hard sip of my drink before I decided whether I should go over there. But what the hell, I talked all this shit, might as well back it up.

I walked confidently towards their table. Did I actually know what I'm going to say? No. I believe that some things can't be planned, you just have to play it by ear.

"Excuse me, good evening, ladies," I said when I finally reached their table.

"Good evening. Can we help you with something?" The one to my left said. I knew she was the more aggressive one out of the bunch. The first one to speak normally is.

"I was hoping so. See, you ladies are beautiful and me and my friends couldn't stop ourselves from staring. So, I was left with a dilemma. Either stand back and let a chance pass by or take a life-changing risk by coming over to introduce myself."

"A life changing risk? Honestly?" The one to my right said, taking her left hand off the table that has a ring on her finger, which showed she was taken.

"Yes, rejection can ruin self-esteem for sure," I said, and they shared a laugh.

"Do you have a name?" The aggressive one asked.

"Adrian," I said to her in a smooth voice. I looked deep into her eyes so she can know that I was serious about whatever was going to happen in the next five minutes.

"You're brave for coming over here, Adrian. I was tempted to send you back where you came from with your chocolate self."

"Sure was. Interrupting our conversation..." the taken one said.

"I sincerely apologize. I'm just a man who has seen something he likes, so I called myself going for it."

"Mmm. I like that in a man, but what did you see that you like over here?" Ms. Aggressive asked, and I knew this was the time I had to choose one.

Mrs. Taken was off limits. I probably had a good shot at Ms. Aggressive, but the entire time I have been over here, the middle women just remained quiet. That made me curious somehow. "To be quite honest, it was you," I said, giving the quiet one eye contact.

"Me?" she asked, kind of surprise like she wasn't an option. "Yes, you. Do you have a name?"

"Sure, so her name is Kelly and I'm Sophia and that's Jerrie," she said, pointing to Ms. Aggressive while Kelly looks at her like she was crazy.

"Are you single, Ms. Kelly?"

"Yes, she is," Sophia answered again for her.

"Is he talking to me or you, Sophia?" Kelly snapped at her.

"Sorry, you know I love you, girl. I'm going to be quiet from here on out. I promise."

I stood there trying to compress my amusement. I dug into my pocket and grabbed one of my business cards. "Listen, I don't want to hold you up. Here's my card in case you decide to call or something. My email is on there too. I hope you ladies enjoy the rest of your evening. Sorry for the interruption," I said as I headed back to my table of friends. As I turned, I couldn't help but smile walking away.

"That easy, huh?" Dominic says when I return.

"They're humans just like us. It's easier to keep things simple, and that's exactly what I did," I told them.

"Man, I want to be like you when I grow up," Jake states as we all share a laugh.

"Alright, come on now. Can we get this party started? We need more drinks, guys. It's been a hard-earned week for all of us."

"AMEN TO THAT!" they all said.

DON'T OVERTHINK
Kelly

"He was handsome, Kelly. Why were you acting all shy, like a little schoolgirl or something?" Jerrie asked while sipping her drink.

"I wasn't acting shy." Truth be told, I was. Every time a guy came over, it was never for me. Jerrie and Sophia were always in the spotlight. Now it was my turn, and I just didn't know what to do with myself.

"Bullshit!" Sophia stated, while slamming her drink down on the table.

"Oh my God," I said, shaking my head. Why was she so mad? Maybe because a guy finally talked to me and not her.

"Kelly, you were quiet as a church mouse. That was a tall glass of chocolate right there with your name on it," Sophia said while licking her lips seductively.

"Umm humm," Jerrie chimed in on the side of me.

First of all, Jerrie is married and Sophia needed to calm down with her horny ass. But they were right. I was just nervous to put myself out there. I'm the type of girl guys overlook all the time. I'm forty years old and haven't been in a relationship in like six years.

"I was a little nervous. I'll admit that." I told them.

"Nervous about what, girl?" Sophia asked me.

"I haven't dated in six years now," I said, hoping that they wouldn't judge me.

"That doesn't mean anything. Do you find him attractive?" Jerrie asked with a stern look on her face.

Of course, I found him attractive. I got eyes. He looked like a good mix between Lance Gross and Kofi Siriboe, and I didn't know if that was even possible to be that fine. "He's handsome but looks are not everything to me. A lot of men don't know how to handle a woman like myself." I said, rubbing my body.

"Yeah, Kelly tell her, girl." Sophia said as she snapped her fingers, hyping me up.

"I'm a career driven and very independent woman. When men find out that I'm a hard, no-nonsense judge, it's intimidating to some of them. The ones it doesn't bother are the ones I'm really not attracted to," I told them while looking down at my water down drink.

"You work in a courthouse with fine ass lawyers. You should snag you one," Jerrie suggested.

If only she knew who my last relationship was with. That's why I stopped putting myself out there. What he did to me was dirty. I promised myself never to take a man seriously just because he looks good.

"When they find out that I'm a judge and I look fairly young, you think that in a male dominated career field they will accept a woman that's doing better than them. Doubt it. Some men's egos and pride are just too big," I stated.

"So, what does his card say he does?" Jerrie asked.

I almost forgot I was holding it in my hand. I looked at it. "It's said he's a real estate agent; Adrian Keller." I looked at the card and all I wanted to do was look it up to see if this was real or fake.

"That's not bad at all, a realtor. Way to go, brother. So, are you going to reach out to him?" Jerrie asked.

"Jerrie!" Sophia says.

"What? I want to know, because if she doesn't, I want to. He shouldn't go to waste… I mean what?" Jerrie said with confidence in the world while forgetting that she was married.

"Jerrie, you're married. Sorry." She looked down at her ring and mouthed fuck to herself. I just realized maybe Sophia wasn't the horny one after all. This was girl is crazy, but that's why I love her.

"Yes, I am going to reach out to him, thank you very much. Hopefully he's not one of those types of people who thinks since he has a good career and money that he can lack in personality," I said.

"Girl, you better than me. I was thinking I hope he's not the type to have a big dick and don't know how to use it," Jerrie stated, and we all laugh.

"Okay ladies let's get out of here," Sophia said as we stood and gather our things after leaving a tip.

It was a good thing too. I was tired and just happy it was the weekend. I sure did plan on contacting Adrian, though. Hopefully, he was different.

SHE'S MINE
Christopher

It was safe to say I was drunk. I was just proud that I made it home safely from OOKA. I really needed a night like this, plus those guys were hysterical. I think I staggered a little as I made it to my front door. I spent more time than usual getting the key in the door, but I got it and entered the house.

All the lights were off besides the hallway light, and I knew it was later than the normal time I get in. I just really needed some time to enjoy myself. I headed to the bathroom to urinate. I guess those drinks were running through me because it seemed like forever before I finally got done. I flushed the toilet and proceeded to the sink to wash my hands and splash some water on my face to try to sober up.

As I towel dried my face, I looked at myself in the mirror. It had been a long night of drinking, but you couldn't tell. I left the bathroom and headed upstairs to check on my princess. I opened up her room door to find her sound asleep.

Siren always made me feel calm and proud to be a father. If Renee and I did nothing else right with Siren, we made sure she was perfect in the eyes of the world. Despite how we felt for one another right now, we both could agree that Siren was our world.

Thinking about how I felt about nut-ass Renee, I felt bad because I hadn't slept in our bed since the situation happened a week and a half ago. I missed her, and I loved her.

I slowly closed Siren's door back and decided to check on my wife. Our door was always open when those two were home by themselves.

I stared at my wife as she slept, her thick thigh sticking out from under the blanket. Renee was beautiful. She used to be skinny, but after Siren, "slim-thick" was the best way to describe her. Now, I loved every inch of her.

Seeing her curves form the blanket made me horny. I wanted her badly. I wanted to make her mine again. I walked over to the bed, taking my shirt off. She wanted the old me and that's exactly what I planned on giving to her.

I slipped the blanket off her as I kissed her on her forehead. She was still. I kissed her lips softly. I kissed her again as I squeezed her ass with my hands until she returned my kisses.

"Where have you been?" she asked, but I ignored her as I rolled her onto her back. I wanted to show her that how much I wanted her. My tongue and hands were the only way I wanted to show my passion for her. I needed her body to understand me and my feelings towards her.

Her hips pushed off the bed as she tried to help my tongue explore deeper into her. I slid along her slit, caressing her clit. I sucked softly at first, then flicked it with my tongue as I dove back down to taste her flowing juices. She was sweet; nothing tasted sweeter.

She placed her hands on my head as I flicked my tongue over her spot. I began to finger fuck her wet opening, making my two fingers penetrate deep as they rubbed against the back of her clitoris.

I wanted her to orgasm, and I planned on taking her there. I moaned and she applied more pressure to the back of my head, forcing me into her. I sped up my pace and deepened my stroke as my fingers penetrated deeper and deeper. She squeezed my head with her thighs and it felt like I was drowning in her as I replaced my tongue with my fingers. I was like a kitten lapping up some milk as I held my breath and rode her to this destination.

When her spasms subsided, she tried to push me away, but I grabbed her hands and kept lapping away. It wasn't about her now; it was about me and I had something to prove. I put my hands in the crooks of her knees and push them to her shoulders as I licked further down to her backdoor. I licked and teased her forbidden place as she squirmed to get away at first, but eventually gave in to me.

I stopped and unfastened my pants. As my boxers dropped to my feet, I stepped out my sneakers. Renee just stared at me with her legs still spread the way I left them. I grabbed one of her legs and pushed it to the side, showing for her to roll over. I didn't want to just make love to her, I wanted to make her mine again.

I pulled her hips until her ass was in the air and searched for her opening as I tried to guide myself into her. When I found her warmth, I knew I was where I needed to be. I missed her sex. I eased into her slowly, feeling how slippery she was and wondered if she missed me. I pushed her away and pulled her back to me, feeling her flesh slap against my own.

I had something to prove, and I thrusted forward feeling myself hit the bottom as she moaned and gasped for air. She's mine and I think she knew it. Our flesh created the beat to my drum. The rhythm continued to play as she moaned and groaned, accepting what I offered by pushing back. Watching her work was hypnotizing; she was like a piece of art, but I couldn't help the vision of her being with another in our bed.

My stroke picks up and so does the beat of the drum. It was a chase, and I was in a hot pursuit.

"Why?" I asked, as I smacked her ass. She didn't answer, just groaned into the pillow clutching the sheets. I needed and deserved an answer. I pulled her harder to me, stroking deeper, working up a sweat. I smacked her ass again and she screamed, "YES!" As she pushed back against me, the chase continued as she evaded me.

The more I gave, the more she was willing to take from me. The beat played on and on. I reached for the back of her neck as I pinned her down. I had to make her submit. My thrusts became more urgent. I looked down, watching her ass ripple from my force that I was administering. She was beautiful, my wife, but my enemy all in one. I couldn't forget that.

My pace slowed down, and then I pulled myself out of her and bent to kiss her opening from that position. I felt sorry for taking my revenge out on her like that. She wiggled her ass against me, as I rolled her back over and climbed on top of her to give her a kiss.

She guided my penis with her hand as she tasted herself from my tongue. When I pushed forth through her warmth this time, I was gentle, wanting to stay close, hold her, and feel her love like I do, but something in me couldn't. I didn't see her as just mine anymore.

I bit her neck as I humped, deeply grinding myself against her when I hit bottom. She responded by holding me, trying to pull me closer to her and the more she did, the more I wanted to get away from her. I rose up, placing her legs over my shoulders, and as I leaned back down, I thrusted forward again. I heard the drums again in the distance, but this time, I noticed it's the one in my chest.

I chased it as she moaned. I drove deep and heard her panting in my ear every turn on the road. I sped to her and the drum was the engine. I felt her near and so was I but I was trying to win this race. I felt it and she grabbed me, letting me know she felt me too. Her body talked to my own, and I grunted, letting my release spill inside of her. She never let go of me. She took everything I had to give until I was empty.

I laid beside her, and she rolled over to face me.

"Please don't, not tonight. Let's just lay here," I say cutting her off before she starts talking.

We laid there in our bed as husband and wife until I fell asleep with her head on my chest.

HENNESSY AND A QUESTION
Renee

I didn't know what got into Christopher last night, but I loved it and enjoyed having my husband back next to me. I was starting to fear the worst after the first few days, let alone a week of him not wanting to share a bed with me.

I started to wake him up for another go this morning but decided against it knowing our daughter, Siren, would be up to watch her Saturday morning cartoons. The first thing that little girl is going to do is run to her father. I wondered where he was last night and was sure to ask him when he gets up.

I got up myself out of bed and took a shower before making breakfast for my family. The feeling of the cool floor made me want to jump right back in bed, but I didn't. I turned on the shower, adjusting the temperature to my liking. Hearing the waterfall must have triggered my bladder because I suddenly had to pee.

I sat on the toilet releasing my bladder as I thought about last night. Chris hadn't done me like that in a while. Forget love making, he took what was his, and I enjoyed the ride. He asked me why and I didn't understand what he meant by that, but my mind wasn't able to think clearly at that time.

I got up and flushed the toilet, took off my night-gown, and stepped into the warm water. It soothed me as I started to lather my body with soap. I loved the feel of my own body, the weight of my breast, and curves of my hips that mother nature blesses me with. I was tempted to rub myself, but there was no need—I had my husband back to fix that problem.

I wish he gave me more of himself often. I want to feel wanted by him like when we were younger and all he wanted to do was sneak off with me and fuck or make love to me.

I admit I was wrong for what happened between me and Sabrina, but it was meant to be enjoyed with him. I just wasn't expecting her mouth to feel so good. I thought he would enjoy the show or at least join in. I didn't want to hurt him, or I wouldn't haven't tried it at all.

I turned the shower off and grabbed a towel to dry off. I wrapped the towel around myself when I finish before brushing my teeth. I wiped the perspiration from the steam off the mirror so I could view myself. I didn't know what it is, but lately I started noticing myself caring more about how I looked. I guess after turning thirty-five, I started caring whether I look my age or not. I stared at my brown skin in the mirror and hated the thought of growing old.

I finished brushing my teeth and rinsed my mouth out before heading back into the bedroom. Chris seemed like he was getting better with age. He came a long way from when we first met. He used to have me snatching them little girls' ponytails out because he wanted to be Mr. Smooth. Then I would run up and down a block beating him and her ass with it.

I giggled to myself at some of those memories as I straddled his waist, trying to wake him.

"If you truly love me, you'll wake up and keep me company," I whisper into his ear.

He stirred, reaching around and grabbing my ass with both hands.

"That's not fair to guilt trip a sleeping man like that," he said.

I nibbled on his ear, and I felt a tingle between my thighs as he grinded against my vagina.

"Don't forget morning breath-" I joked. "I want to talk, baby. I miss you and I'm sorry."

"I don't want to talk about that, Renee. Let's just let it go for now," he protested. I want to keep him in a good mood, so I let it go.

"So, what do you want to talk about then?" I asked him.

"This." He squeezed my ass cheeks, and I felt his erection press up against me.

"Last night was great, but where were you?" I questioned.

"I went to OOKA with the fellas. I had a few drinks and got something to eat," he told me.

"So that explains it. Then you came home and gave me some henny dick…" I accused him.

"I didn't hear any complaints last night," he countered.

"Because there wasn't none," I said as I slid down his body until I'm face to face with his brown skin. I grabbed it, pulling the foreskin back as I stroke him right before lowering my mouth down over the tip. He let out a sigh as I worked more of him into my mouth until we heard footsteps coming fast.

I quickly jumped to the side of the bed as he snatched the covers over him just before the door swung open and our six-year-old daughter came running into our bedroom.

"Siren!" I yelled. "Stop all that running in my house!"

"Daddy!" she screamed, ignoring me like I didn't matter or count for nothing as she ran to his side of the bed.

"Hey princess! Good morning," Christopher said, petting her head.

"Good morning, Daddy. Where were you last night? You didn't tuck me in," Siren questioned like the sweet little kid she is.

"I was out with Uncle Adrian. It's all his fault. We got to give him a piece of our mind, don't we?" Siren nodded enthusiastically.

"Come on Siren. Let's give your dad some time to get up while we go make him some breakfast. You going to be my little helper or what?" I asked, trying to put some shorts and a tank top on.

"Yeah!" she said beating me to the door. I followed her and before I left, I looked back at my husband and said "Maybe next time" before closing the door behind me.

NOTHING BUT BUSINESS
Kelly

Here I was, an honorable judge who makes decisions that will change a person's life every day, and I was nervous and skeptical about doing something that might change mine.

I don't know what I found so hard about contacting a man that I find attractive but making that phone call just seemed too difficult to initiate. What if he didn't like me or think of me as an attractive woman. But then I looked at his business card and obviously he already made that clear that he does because no man is going to give his information to someone unattractive. I guess I really didn't want to waste my time.

I leaned back in my chair at my office desk. It was a busy day in my courtroom and I was happy that my eight hours were up, but I couldn't help that Adrian was on my mind most of the time.

Should I call him or not? Will he answer me? Wait, does he even remember me? What happens if he answers, what will I say? Pull yourself together Kelly, it's just a man.

I decided what the hell and went for it. I reached for my cell phone and dialed the number on the business card that was in my hand. I decided to go all the way through but heard the first ring and hung up. I couldn't form words. Oh, thank God he had an email. Emailing him gave me time to think before I actually had to respond.

Send to: AdrianKeller@gmail.com

From: KellyPatten@montco.com [4:51 pm]

Hi, I just wanted to reach out to you. We met at the OOKA restaurant, remember?

I figured that would be enough until he checks his emails. I don't know why, but I was anticipating his response. I felt kind of giddy like a kid waiting for recess to have time to run and play. But no immediate response followed, and I was kind of disappointed.

I gathered up my things to get ready to leave. This disappointment was the reason why I didn't miss dating or putting myself out there. I felt like you give control over to someone to disappoint you. It's like extending your hand for a handshake for it to be just left out there. It's embarrassing and makes you not want to try it again.

I head out of the office to catch the elevator and get out of there. "Hey, your honor," the Sheriff said to me when I stepped in the elevator.

"How was your day, Sheriff?" I asked. He was usually the sheriff assigned to my courtroom.

"Just another day at work," he stated pressing the button for the ground level.

"I hear that." I said with a chuckle.

The elevator took off and we are quiet for the ride down. Finally, we reached the ground level and the doors slid open.

"Ladies first, your honor."

"Thank you. Nice to know we still have gentlemen in the world," I said, walking off and soon, I was walking out on the busy streets of Swede and Airy.

It took a moment to get to my car because I had to park far from the courthouse. I couldn't wait to get in my car, put my sweats on, and forget about today. Jerrie told me to do one day, so I guess today was the day.

I started my royal blue 2019 BMW M5 and a part of me always felt proud driving her around town. It made me feel like I could compete with my male counterpart in my career. My car meant a lot to me and people who knew me knew it.

I pulled off into traffic to head home to Lola, my three-year-old Saint Bernard. I didn't stay far from the courthouse; I lived in Collegeville, PA in a nice four bedrooms, two-and-a-half-bathroom home.

The ride home went by fast as I found myself pulling up into the driveway in no time. I couldn't wait to sip some wine and catch up on the rest of *Power*.

As I unlocked my front door, Lola bolted to her favorite tree to use the bathroom. I waited for her to get done as she ran to me and then back inside the house. After I fed Lola, I heated up some leftover spaghetti.

My cell phone went off and I checked my notifications. I had an email from Adrian. My heartbeat throbbed and my nerves got to me as I opened it.

Send to: KellyPatten@montco.com

From: AdrianKeller@gmail.com [5:37 pm]

Sorry I was in a meeting. Of course, I remember exactly who you are. The quiet one at the table. I'm happy to hear from you.

"OH, MY FUCKING GOD! HE REMEMBERS ME! Ok Kelly, calm down."

That got me excited as I took a seat on the couch almost spilling my wine.

"Shoot I got to respond, but what should I say? Lola, I need your help. How can I say let's go on a date without letting him know I want a date?"

I looked at Lola as she looked at me and continued to eat her food. "You're no help." I put my wine down and think of something to say.

Send to: AdrianKeller@gmail.com

From: KellyPatten@montco.com [5:41 pm]

I am glad to hear from you as well. I thought you forgot about me. So how was your day?

Send to: KellyPatten@montco.com

From: AdrianKeller@gmail.com [5:42 pm]

My day has been kind of busy. I have another meeting in about a half an hour. Are you free this weekend? We could probably do lunch.

Yes, I'm free on the weekend! I just can't let you know that.

Send to: AdrianKeller@gmail.com

From: KellyPatten@montco.com [5:43 pm]

I'm not actually sure yet if I am available this weekend. It's too early to tell. Maybe later on in the week I'll let you know. But I will email you and keep you posted.

Send to: KellyPatten@montco.com

From: AdrianKeller@gmail.com [5:44pm]

That's smooth, but please don't think too hard. I have to go prepare for my next client. I'll check back in later to see if your schedule becomes clear.

Send to: AdrianKeller@gmail.com

From: KellyPatten@montco.com [5:45 pm]

Sounds like a plan. I wish you well with your client.

I put my phone down and before it goes off again.

Send to: KellyPatten@montco.com

From: AdrianKeller@gmail.com [5:46pm]

Thanks.

That was easier than I thought, but for some reason, it gave me butterflies. Maybe that was just my stomach because I ate three-day old spaghetti. I grab my bottle of wine to finish off because I knew how my night was about to end. *Power,* here I come.

Christopher

I couldn't believe what me and Adrian stumbled upon as we stepped inside the back office of Set It Off. Set It Off was one of our business adventures we started when we first came into some real money. It was an erotic bar, but since Adrian and I were too busy to handle the day to day work we decided to let my cousin, Matthew, take over and be commander and chief. It was a good idea up until the moment I saw them.

Matt had our bartender bent over the office desk and was pounding her back out.

"Matt! What the fuck, man!" I barked as they scrambled to pull their clothes together.

"When the hell did this become a part of business?" I asked. I was furious, and I could only imagine what Adrian was thinking about in the situation.

"I'm sorry, Chris. It's all my fault," Matt said as he fastened his belt. Amour quickly exited the room, trying to keep her head down to avoid eye contact with me.

"You think?" Adrian said as he took a seat in the chair in front of the desk.

"I know. Something came over me man and it just happened. I mean did you look at her? It won't happen again," Matt said.

"Damn right it won't. She is not going to be around for it to happen again," I told him.

"Come on Chris, you don't have to fire the chick, man." Matt said to me as he finished cleaning himself up.

"The same way you didn't have to fuck the bitch, Matt. But guess the fuck what? Something came over me," I scoffed.

Matt was my younger cousin and back before I ever did any jail time, we used to hustle together. After Matt was shot for going across town to deal with a chick that belonged to someone we did business with, he took a step back from that lifestyle. He clearly couldn't keep his hormones in check.

"Let's just get down to business," Adrian finally said, breaking the tension in the room. "Do you have this month's payment Matt?"

"Of course, Ad. You know I'll never mess no cash up. Plus, this was dropped off by Weegy yesterday," Matt said, picking up a bag from under his desk and tossing it to me.

I checked the contents of the bag and nodded to Adrian as I thumbed through bands of money.

"It looks like everything," I said.

"Weegy never did me wrong in business, so I don't expect him to," Adrian said as he stared at Matt. "And what about our share?"

"Already deposited," Matt said, while passing the bank receipt over to Adrian.

"Well, everything checks out Ad. Let's get out of here." I said, as I headed toward the door.

"I'm disappointed in you Matt, seriously. It's like you don't learn, man." I said before leaving the office. I saw Amour behind the bar and decided to give her a piece of my mind before I left.

"Amour listen, I like you as a person, but don't lose your job over because you're horny. I was real close to firing you," I told her.

"Oh, but it was okay when you were fucking me a couple years back, huh?" she countered back.

"Abso-fucking-lutely because you weren't working for me. I'm not here to belittle you or anything. I'm just saying, keep business strictly business or leave and never come back," I told her as I continued out the door.

"I hear you," she said in a sassy tone.

"Well hear this then. Get your shit and get the fuck out, you hear that!" I snapped on her. I didn't have time for this with a woman who didn't belong to me.

I faded into a daydream but quickly snapped out of it when Adrian tapped me on my shoulder. I was watching Amour gather her shit as she made a big deal, stomping her feet with every step.

"Amour, you don't have to leave. Just get it together, seriously." I said, as I headed out the front door to my car.

I placed the bag in the trunk of my car when my cell phone started vibrating. I looked down and saw I had a text message from Renee telling me to call her when I got a chance. I walked over to Adrian's car and told him, "Look man, I'm just going to catch up to you later. I got to check Renee and see what's up. I'll just meet up with you at the spot later if that's good with you."

"Go ahead and handle yours, and I'll get with you. I honestly have something I got to do myself, so we're good," he said to me.

I gave him some dap before we departed and as soon as I hopped into my car, I got Renee on the phone.

"Renee, what's wrong?" I said with a concerned tone. "Just come home," she said with a sigh in her voice.

BEING NERVOUS
Kelly

I had agreed to meet Adrian for lunch and I was a bit nervous. We were supposed to be meeting at Olive Garden in downtown center city, but I was running late because I couldn't decide on what to wear.

As I drove around looking for a parking spot, I couldn't help but wonder if I looked good enough or smelled nice and that he doesn't stand me up. I knew Adrian had his shit together, so I had to bring my A game. I quickly spotted a parking spot that snapped me back to reality.

I finally made it and squeezed in that small parking space. As I walked down Broad Street heading towards the restaurant, I felt confident in my appearance. I had on a $1,200 navy blue pinstripe two-piece business suit by Jonathan Simkai, a white Philanthropy bodysuit and a pair of white Chloe Gosselin leather ankle boots to match plus some accessories with a gold necklace and a $2,000 Salvatore Ferragamo handbag.

You couldn't tell me I wasn't the hottest woman walking down the street. I saw Adrian sitting at the table and added a sway in my walk. Damn he looked good.

"Hey handsome. Mind if I join you?" I asked as I took a seat.

"Sure, but hello to you, beautiful." he said to me, which put a smile on my face.

"How long did I keep you waiting? I'm so sorry please forgive me." I said with a concerned look on my face.

"About fifteen minutes and it's not a big deal. It helped me get over my nerves," he told me while looking down at his phone.

"So, you were nervous?" I asked, eyeing him.

"I was, but any man would've been. You're breathtaking," he said, staring into my eyes which gave me butterflies. Damn. He was good.

"That's very flattering. You're such a smooth talker, aren't you?" I said while I was looking over the menu.

"More like a sincere one," he said to me while taking a sip of water.

Something about him just seemed serious and mysterious all at the same time. Plus, the way he gazed at me made me uneasy and nervous.

The server approached the table, saving me from my own thoughts.

"Hello I'm Paula. I'll be your waiter this afternoon. Are you two ready to place your orders, or would you like more time?" she asked with a pleasant smile.

"That's up to the lady," Adrian said as I glanced over the menu again to make sure what I order was what I want.

"I would like a chicken alfredo in a garlic bread bowl please."

"And to drink?" the waitress asked.

"If you can recommend some red wine that would be fine," I told her. As I'm looked at her, I can feel his eyes on me. I wondered what he was thinking. He probably thought he was going to get some after this. Olive Garden for some pussy? You got to do better than that, and I don't care how good you look.

"Chardonnay or Merlot?" she said.

"Merlot if you can please," I told her hoping that she would give me a hefty pour to calm my nerves.

"Okay and for you sir? The waitress said, turning to Adrian.

"I'll take the same as her just make my drink a chardonnay," he told her with a smile on his face. Was this a test to see what kind of person I am? He probably thought I was going to order a salad or something else light.

"Okay, I'll have it for you as soon as possible. Please enjoy yourself," she said before walking off.

"She seems nice," I stated, referring to the waitress.

"I agree, but back to us. I'm glad that you agreed to have lunch with me today. I thought you might be busy," Adrian tells me.

"I figured I could make some room to enjoy myself. I honestly don't get out much," I said to him, hoping he wouldn't think all I did was work and sleep.

"I believe you will," he said, gazing at me again. "What do you do for a living, if you don't mind me asking."

"I'm a judge." I can tell Adrian was shocked by my response by his facial expression.

"You're kidding?"

I shook my head no. "Very serious," I said while looking around for the drinks to come. He regained his composure as we fell silent for a second. Where were those drinks?

"Wow, sorry I just didn't ever think that would be your answer. I didn't know a judge could actually be so young," he said while looking me up and down.

"Anything is possible with hard work and ambition on your side," I stated.

"I know that's right!" he responded back. We fell silent again for a moment until Adrian spoke. "So, can you help me understand something?" he asked me.

"Sure," I said with a concerned look on my face. What was it that he was going to ask me? What made you become a judge? What kind of cases do you handle? Bring on the bullshit questions.

"Why are you still single?" he asked me in the smoothest voice ever, sounding like melted butter to my ears.

"Who said I am?" I countered back trying to keep a serious face to mess with him. "Just kidding, I have no idea. I guess most men are a bit intimidated when it comes to my career."

"You had me kind of worried for a second," he admitted while jokingly holding his chest.

"No need to be worried, but I can ask you the same. Why are you still single?" I asked.

He looked like he was pondering the thought in his head shifting it from one side to the other before speaking.

"I guess I could say because I haven't actually found exactly what I like or want in a woman yet." He looked sincere, but that didn't cure my skepticism.

"Kids?"

"What about them?" I wanted to know if I had to worry about baby mama drama and how many baby mamas you have.

"Do you have any?" I asked him, while looking straight in his eyes.

"No, I don't want no baby mamas running around driving me crazy. How about yourself?" he asked.

"None yet, maybe one day," I said while moving my hair out of my face.

"I know this may be off topic, but I'm very curious to know. How have you ever dated an African American man before?" he asked. I was hoping that he was joking with me. I dated all kinds of people and didn't care what race they were.

"You mean a black man?" I asked frankly. I couldn't believe that question or maybe I just wasn't expecting it. I mean it wasn't everyday someone asked me if I date black men.

"Well yes."

"Once in college. Is that a problem? Better yet have you ever dated a white woman?" I shot back.

He smirked. "To be honest, no. Don't get me wrong, I don't want you feeling offended nor like you have to be defensive. I'm straight forward, so if I'm curious about something I'll ask about it. I have never been down this road before, so I wanted to know, have you?"

I let his words sink in and the waitress just so happened to bring us our food.

"Here you guys are. I'll be right back with y'all's bottles of wine," she said as she hurried back to the bar.

"So, tell me Mr. Keller what it is that you might like or want in a woman?" I asked, wanting to know did I fit anywhere in the category.

The waitress came back placing two wine glasses on the table along with two bottles of wine, before she asked if we needed anything else. I shook my head telling her no with a smile on my face.

Adrian spoke, "I just want something different. Something that's not so formal, but most people are so custom," He said while popping the merlot for me open.

"By that you mean?"

"I want a woman who is adventurous and not afraid to lust without limits," He said to me while sipping his wine and looking deep into my eyes.

That threw me for a loop for a split second. "So, you mean to tell me it's all about sex for you…"

He looked at me as he took a fork full of alfredo noodles into his mouth. I waited for him to finish as he dabbed his mouth before he spoke again.

"Some might say that, but no, that's not what I mean when I say adventurous. I mean someone who is not afraid to take a chance. Someone who is not afraid of judgement. A lot of people these days care too much about what others think instead of what they feel. That's what I meant by that."

"So, what about not being afraid to lust without limits? What do you mean by that?" As I waited for his response, I realized how good my food is or I must have been really hungry.

"Lust for me. I want admiration and appreciation. When you noticed me watching you approach, you started to walk with more of a sway in your hips than you did before. I admired and appreciated the extra energy. I thought about how much more energy you are willing to give to something or someone who you have found to be worth it."

I listened to his words and to say I wasn't intriguing would be a lie. I just took a bite and sip some wine to wash it down. I looked up to find him doing the same. He was more handsome than I remembered and seemed to be intelligent just as well.

"Are you a player?" I had to ask. He just seemed like he could talk his way into a woman's panties.

"No, I don't believe in having multiple relationships; one is enough for me if and when I finally decide to have one," he answered.

We continued to eat until we were finished our conversation, and though the conversation was short, the words hit like a ton of bricks.

"Are you ready to go?" Adrian asked me.

"Unfortunately, yes I believe so." I gathered my things and offered to pay for my half of the meal, but he told me it was already taken care of and offered to walk me to my car.

I hadn't noticed how small I was compared to him until I was walking right beside him. I felt those butterflies coming back, and I didn't understand what caused them. It might be because I didn't want our time to just end yet. I didn't know what came over me with this man.

"Do you treat all first dates like this?" I asked him as we reached my car.

There was that smirk again. "I told you, I don't do formal things usually. I don't even remember the last time I had a first date. Especially a formal one," he said to me with his hands in his pockets. He looked like he had something else on his mind but what was it? Looking up at him, I figured I would just be frank with him.

"Are you just trying to have sex with me?" I asked him with a straight face. He laughed and I felt kind of embarrassed for saying such a thing out loud. "Nevermind. Please just forget it. I'm sorry to insult you in that way."

"No. No. No. It's okay, I'd rather hear the bluntness. Remember what I said about being adventurous. It just caught me off guard and made me laugh honestly," he said while taking a step closer to me invading my personal space.

"I'll always be honest with you. Did I plan on having sex with you? Of course, if we reach that point, but that depends on you. It's not an objective of mine." I could feel nothing but wetness in my panties. My throat became dry with him being so close to me. I could smell him, hear his heartbeat, catch the rhythm of his breathing.

"Are you willing or planning on going there with me?" he asked.

My nerves were on fire throughout my body and I had to remind myself to talk. "We're grown, so I'll admit that would be nice, but I'm not no hot in the pants type of woman," I told him, even though I was.

"I'm not asking you to be. You don't have to be any of that. I just need you to be willing," he told me.

"Willing to what?" I asked, damn near gasping for air.

"Willing to be free with me," he stated only inches away from my face.

"How do I do that?"

"Kiss me," he said while holding me chin.

"What! Why? What will that prove?" I asked thinking that he lost his mind.

He said, "Everything."

Christopher

I rushed home after receiving Renee's text message and phone call. I jumped out of my car as soon as I put it in park and rushed to the front door.

As I stepped into the house I came face to face with Siren and her friend, Zya, who was about Siren's age.

"Daddy!" my daughter yelled as she ran up to give me a hug like I had been gone forever.

"Hey there, princess. You missed me, I see," I said picking her up.

"Yeah, where did you go?" she asked me.

"Just had to go take care of some things. I'm home now to spend all the time I have with you," I said as I walked with her back over to where Zya was sitting.

"Hey, Zya. I get no love from you?" I asked while bending down next to her as she reached over to give me a hug. "So, what are you little girls doing being alone here?"

"Playing," Siren answered with a slight chuckle. I couldn't help but stare at the two. They look so similar in ways, but I guess all kids do.

"I'll be back. Where is mommy?"

"Out back on the porch," Zya said, playing some game on Siren's tablet.

I left them to their games and headed off to find their mothers. I couldn't wait to see Renee to find out what this emergency was all about. I heard them on the porch out back before I opened the screen door.

"I'm telling you girl, just watch. It's not going to end well with that Porsha and the hot dog man," Erin stated.

"Girl, you always think negative. That girl finally found her happiness. Let her be," Renee scoffed.

"I'll be happy too; I never go hungry again. I'll eat all of them hot dogs too, if you know what I mean," Erin said before I let my presence be known.

"Excuse me, but Renee, can I talk to you for a second." I asked startling them as they looked back over their shoulders. Erin greeted me, but I tried my best to avoid her and gave her a dry acknowledgement.

"Well, I'm just going to go check on the kids and give y'all a chance to talk," Erin said getting up.

I couldn't help but notice her ass in the leggings she was wearing. Erin might have been white, but her body was Black. That was part of the reason I tried my best to avoid her. When she was out of eyeshot of us, I got right to the point.

"What's going on? What was the emergency?" I asked looking around the back yard, making sure I wasn't missing anything.

"Your daughter. She is the emergency. Siren has been asking about you all morning since you left. What the hell am I supposed to tell her. You are not at work and I'm not lying to my child. There shouldn't be any reason why you're not at home on a Saturday spending time with your wife and an only child," she said with a roll of her neck. Why does she have an attitude? I'm here, right? That should matter, but to Renee, it doesn't.

"Come on, Renee, you can't be serious," I said in disbelief that she said that this was an emergency.

"I'm very fucking serious. Luckily Erin brought Zya over to keep her company. Where did you go anyway, Christopher? You better not be up to your old tricks again. Don't let me find out you are creeping. I'm getting too old to be beating these little bitches' asses out here…" Renee ranted on, but I couldn't help but think of those days. Renee got a mean right hook that I never wanted to be on the other end of.

"Renee, can you shut the fuck up with that bullshit?" I told her while rubbing my face.

"You shut up! Don't tell me shut the fuck up. I'm grown!" she said snapping her neck again.

"Renee, please. Calm down, Renee. You're tripping," I said looking over my shoulder making sure Erin couldn't hear us.

"So where were you then?" she questioned. I sighed. I couldn't believe what I walked into.

"I was with Adrian handling something," I confessed.

"That's always your excuse. Adrian this or Adrian that, you're not slick. I can see through that bullshit. That's the reason you came in one or two o'clock in the morning wanting to jump all on me huh? Please! You're full of shit," she said to me. Why do I have to be full of shit? I'm telling her the truth.

"I'm being honest, Renee," I said shrugging my shoulders.

"Well, even if you are telling the truth, that only means you're up to something. You have no business doing whatever you're doing in the first place, and I don't have time to be visiting no one in prison again, Christopher. We're not young anymore," she said to me while holding my face in her hand.

"Don't you think I know that? You called me for a damn lecture? Accusing me of cheating and shit like I didn't just catch you with your feet to the fucking ceiling. My daughter wanted me and I'm here now. Plus, it's not even like that. We were collecting money from the bar. A business we own – a business in your name," I snapped back at her making her feel like the bad guy for once.

"Don't make this about me," Renee stated while waving her hand and finger in my face.

"I'm not! Just get off my back. I'm doing my best for us," I said, while walking back into the house.

As I entered, I saw Erin in the dining room probably listening to every word we said.

She looked at me as I walked by before she said, "Whenever you get a chance can we talk?"

"Sure, just not right now," I said as I headed upstairs to clear my thoughts and calm my temper.

UNDER HIS CONTROL
Kelly

"This is a beautiful house," I said stepping inside Adrian's home.

"Thanks," he said, not even looking back at me.

"It's a five bedroom and bath, modern colonial, enhanced in 2017. It has a new roof, exterior paint, and landscaping. An open and split floor plan. Ebony wood and marble floors, a butler's pantry, impeccable wood, and granite kitchen. Family and living room. Lushly landscaped brick-pave pool, patio and more." Adrian explained as we entered what I guessed to be the family room.

"Wow. You know all of that? You were speaking like a true realtor," I told him as he tried to suppress a laugh.

"I guess that's a habit. My apologies," he said to me while he looked around his home.

"You don't have to. You are passionate about what you do. I see no wrong in that." I stood in the middle of the room as he headed to the kitchen to retrieve two bottles of water. "Do you actually stay here much?"

"What made you ask that?" Adrian asked while bringing me a bottle of water. "Feel free to sit if you like."

"It just seems very neat to be a house of a bachelor," I admitted as he stood in front of me.

"I'm going to take that as a compliment, but to be honest with you, I only come here when I need to clear my head and get a moment of peace."

"Well, it was a compliment," I assured him, "but what a luxury to have. How much would this house go for?" I inquired.

"1.8 million dollars on today's market. I purchased it for only $975,000 four years ago." Adrian informed me. "Now can I ask you a question?"

"Sure" I told him. I still couldn't get over the fact that this house is 1.8 million. There was no way a man like himself could buy a house like this. He must have a double life or something.

"How do you feel at this very moment?" he asked, gazing at me once again.

I felt nervous as hell. Here I was at this man house who kissed me for the first time today and that I barely even knew. I felt myself giving into him with such ease that it freaked me out, but I couldn't fight it.

"I'm fine," I heard myself say.

He smirked before walking away. "You shouldn't lie, Kelly. Communication is everything."

"Where are you going?" I asked him as he continued to walk away. Lord, what am I getting myself into.

"Be right back." He said as he headed out of the room.

How could he tell I was lying? Was I really that easy to read? I asked myself. My nerves were evident from how my right hand shook. *I really need to snap out of it* I told myself I took a seat to wait on Adrian to return. When he does, he's holding what appears to be a red slick scarf.

"What's that for? I asked.

"You." I didn't know whether to be scared or turned on. "I brought this out for you. Do you mind standing?" He asked while standing a few inches away from myself.

As I stood to my feet, I could hear a thumping sound in my ear. We stood face to face when he started to speak to me.

"Now I'm going to ask you again. Are you willing to try something different, Kelly?" I didn't know what effect he had over me, but I felt weak and dizzy. There was something about him, the way he looked at me – it somewhat allured me.

"Yes. I'm willing." What was I saying? I was ready to get a strange man to have complete control over me. I never had this feeling before.

"Turn around then," he commanded.

"Why?" I asked. What is he trying to do to me? Do I want to see where this goes? Am I up for this now? For him, I'll try.

"Only one way to find out," he whispered in my ear. I couldn't think straight because my panties were overflowing with excitement.

I think about it for a second before reluctantly turning around. A few seconds went past before I felt the scarf coming down over my eyes, blinding me as he tied it behind my head. If I thought I was nervous before, that feeling just magnified by three.

"Now what?" I asked, wanting to know where he was going with this. It was quiet, but I knew he was there.

"I'm going to have you strip. Is that okay with you?"

"You had to blindfold me to do so?" I asked him. He lifted my chin. Placing a kiss on my lips.

"No, but it's more interesting this way for now," he said and removed his hand away from my flesh. My skin still tingled from my chin and lips.

"I need an answer though," he stated. I could tell he was circling me. I was his prey, and he was the hungry predator waiting to eat. He waited for my approval. My breathing became more labored. My chest felt tight, but I managed to choke out my confirmation.

"It's okay." It was quiet again and this time I didn't even hear his footsteps. "Adrian?"

Silence filled the air before he finally spoke.

"I'm here."

"What are you doing?" I asked.

"Watching you," he said as I felt something press against my stomach and move down. He unbuttoned my business suit jacket. I swallowed the lump in my throat and soon I felt my jacket being removed from my body.

I never felt like this before. I felt like I was stuck between fight or flight, which left me to do nothing. Surrendering – that's how I felt. I was surrendering to him, or was I surrendering to myself? I felt him unstrap my boots.

"Lift," he said and I lifted my foot and stepped out my left boot then my right. I felt the carpet on my feet. It was comfortable, soft, and rich.

"Take off your pants, Kelly," he directed me and it sent goose bumps down my arms. I didn't know when I would give up, but I did what he asked of me. I unzipped my pants, lowered them to the ground, and then felt the air on the skin.

"You have nice legs," Adrian said in my ear, startling me. "But you should take off the rest."

I did what he asked, and I was left standing there naked and extremely nervous. I haven't been naked in front of a man in years.

"You have a great body," Adrian said as if he could read my concerns.

"Thank you, but now what?" I asked him. I felt kind of silly just standing there naked and not being able to see anything.

"Just be patient," Adrian said while grabbing me from behind and pulling me into him. I didn't know when he came out of his shirt, but his chest and abs on my back made the wetness continue to flow through my legs even more.

"Mmm," I moaned as he caressed my breast before turning me around. I felt his warm mouth on my left breast first. The warmth and the way his tongue against my nipple felt made my vagina throb as I cradle the back of his head. He continued for a moment then switched to the right one. I missed this closeness with a man.

"Tell me what you want, Kelly."

"Take me. That's what I want," I pant. "I want all of you that you can give me." I answered.

With that being said, I felt myself being pulled forward a couple of steps until we suddenly stopped.

"I'm going to need you to follow my instructions. Can you handle that?" he asked.

"Yes," I said with no hesitation.

"Good," he whispered to me as he began moving behind me. "Bend over."

His tone was demanding. I leaned forward feeling, what I believe to be the cushion from the sofa.

"More, show yourself to me," he told me as I lean downed with my face touching the cushion. I felt myself being exposed for him to see.

I felt the breeze on my vagina as his hands caressed, squeezed and kneading, my cheeks. I couldn't believe I was allowing myself to be groped like this by a stranger.

"Oh my Jesus!" I managed to say as I felt the air fill my lungs as his hot tongue made contact with my slit. It was so satisfying; I arched my back like an alley cat, not wanting him to stop. I felt light-headed and I had to remember to breathe as his tongue lapped away firmly at my sweet spot.

I pushed back against his face and got shocked with a smack to my right ass cheek.

"I control this pace," he said as he turned me over and spread my legs as he drove back into my vagina head first.

"This feels so good." I stated, while feeling my orgasm building in my pelvis. A few seconds after he stopped.

"Jesus Christ, why?" I manage to breathe out as he suddenly stopped just before my release.

He grabbed me by the thighs, bringing me to the edge of the couch before I could feel him place his manhood against my opening. He said nothing. He just rested there for a moment before I felt him pressing into me.

"Oh shit! Mmm!" I moaned as I felt him stretch me open. I didn't know if it was because it had been awhile or if he was really just that big.

"Relax," he told me as he fed me more of himself.

"Jesus Christ, fuck!" I said, gasping for air. It was definitely him. He was big and it hurt as I adjusted to his size. He pulled back again, but this time pushing deeper inside me.

"Aah yes!" I said grabbing him needing the touch of his skin against my own. He picked up the tempo, stroking me deeper and deeper working my vagina. I felt my wetness as his strong body pushed forward.

He stroked me and I tried my best to meet him for every stroke and every time, I felt the base of his dick rub against my clitoris, bringing me to orgasm. I wanted him to take me over the edge–I needed him too. *I needed this* I think to myself as I grabbed him, trying to hold on for the ride as my climax peaked.

It did nothing but stirred him on as he drove into me with more of a passion.

"Yes, yes, fuck! Ooo fuck me!" I yelled, as I felt my muscles contract and my orgasm started to pour out of me. "Ahhh shit! Shit, shit! Yes, yes!" I groaned as Adrian continued to work my body. My vagina was so sensitive as he stroked deeply, making me roll into another orgasm.

"Oh my god! Oh my god. Shit Jesus Christ!" I yelled trying to move away, but his grip wouldn't let me which caused me to dig my nails into his skin. I never came back-to-back like that in my life and I had no control.

"Wait, wait please stop. I need a moment," I managed to tell him. His pace slowed down until he finally stopped.

"Are you okay?" he asked while pulling himself out of me. Immediately, I began craving the pressure inside of me again.

"Yeah, I'm okay. Just very sensitive down there. I just need a moment," I explained.

"That's okay," he said, sitting down next to me. "Was I being rough?"

"No," I answered, squeezing my thighs together to subside my post orgasmic sensation. "It's just been a while for me."

"Oh," Is all he can say as he pulls me on top of him. I straddled his body feeling his chest and abdomen against my body. He was hot, almost as if he was running a fever. I felt him reach around me and soon felt him sliding back in me and I groaned.

My hips took on a mission of their own as I pushed down on him, wanting more as I grinded up and down on top of him. He kissed me and I returned it passionately as I humped his dick.

He grabbed my ass, guiding me up and down on top of him as my clit grinded against his pelvis or the base of his cock.

"Yes! Mmm!" I groaned while working myself to another orgasm.

He grabbed me, pressing my breast against him as he took over and fucked me deeper. He pulled me down as he thrusted up. I get caught off guard as he dug in me. I humped back, wanting everything he had to give. I squeezed my vagina muscles around his dick as we flowed together.

The only sound in the room was our moans and our skin slapping each other. He finally pulled me down on top of him and held me there as I felt the warmth of his seeds spill into my womb. I knew I should have protested, but the feeling was good at the moment that I just rested against him, enjoying the moment.

SNAKES ARE NOT YOUR FRIEND
Renee

I had just gotten back to my workstation after checking in on Mrs. Zimmerman. She was a resident of Jefferson hospital and she got on my damn nerves every ten minutes by constantly paging me. *I just need this day to hurry up because it's just one of those days that I definitely didn't want to be here* I thought to myself as I took a seat and put my headphones back in.

"I'm back now," I stated into my microphone headset. I was on the phone with Erin trying to pass the time.

"Was everything okay?" she asked.

"That old lady getting on my last nerve. She just called me to help her to the bathroom. Like grandma, your legs not the fuck broke it's a couple feet away," I said as Erin laughed at me.

"Girl, you so ignorant. Stop being like that. She probably uses a cane or something," she said with a chuckle.

"I got her damn medical file; she doesn't need no damn cane. When these people find out they have someone who is going to be attentive to them, some of them take advantage of it. I like to see your little snow-white ass come down here and give these old, perverted men a sponge bath. They get off on that shit," I said to her, trying to hold back a laugh.

"If I'm getting paid like you do for it, shit I might enjoy it too," Erin stated, and we both shared a laugh. She was a hot mess.

"Anyway, back to our conversation before we were interrupted. I know his ass up to something. I just can't put my finger on it yet."

"I really think you're wrong on that one. Chris is a great husband to you, Renee. I mean we both know that he loves you--" she was telling me all the things I wanted to hear but right now I just need a friend.

"Damn, are you my friend or his lawyer? I don't need you in my ear trying to protect his integrity or making me think I'm going crazy," I snapped.

"Calm down, Renee. It's not even like that. I just know how you are, and I don't want you to be going backwards in time on me," she said.

"I know that's right, but if I remember correctly, you always out do me when it comes to showing your ass," I told her after I calmed down. Maybe I was being to harsh with her. She was just my friend looking out for me.

Erin laughed. "That's because I need to make my presence known. You know, since I'm a short, white girl they think I'm sweet. I got to go all out so a bitch and her stinking ass friends think twice next time they see me," she said with conviction.

"I heard that," I replied as my supervisor approached. I dared this bitch to speak to me. She thought she was hot shit and I knew she was the sneaky ass one who kept writing me up.

"Hello! Renee?" I heard Erin say.

"I'm here. My supervisor just walked past that's all but look I'm going to go before I end up having to curse her ass out," I told her.

"You still want me to get the girls, or what?" Erin asked.

"More than likely, yeah. Chris is off today but who knows what he's doing. I'm going to go though. Talk to you when I leave," I told her as I disconnected the call.

I looked at the computer screen and saw another resident was in distress. I swear, sometimes I hated my job.

"It's going to be a long day."

Christopher

Thump, thump, thump.

I heard a disturbance from my bedroom, waking me up. I looked over at the clock checking to see the time.

"Oh my God!" I said resting my head back against the pillow. It was 10:48 in the morning. I overslept.

Thump, thump, thump.

I heard the banging again, and I realize it was the front door. Something in me thought about ignoring it, but against my better judgement I tossed the covers back and headed downstairs.

"Who is it!?" I called out as I approached the door.

"Erin!" I heard her say and thought, *what the hell does she think she's doing here?*

I opened the door to find her standing there, and without an invitation, she marched right past me. I stood there for a moment longer than I needed, contemplating whether or not I should tell her about herself, but I let it go and closed the front door.

"What's up Erin, something wrong?" I wondered what this was all about. She stood there shifting all her weight to one side before she actually speaks.

"That's what I'm here to figure out for myself."

"What? What are you talking about?" I asked, yawning but still taken aback.

"Don't play stupid. I heard y'all arguing the other day," she said with a concerned look on her face.

"Okay, and that's none of your business," I said moving past her and heading upstairs to the bathroom. She followed right behind me.

"What the hell you mean it's none of my business, Chris? Just because my name is not Renee, what you're doing out there in the streets and who you do it with makes it my business. Plus, as long as you're fucking me and sharing my bed, I have the right to know as well as her. It's bad enough you're married, not only that but to my best friend," she said to me while I tried to get myself ready for my day.

I turned on the water and brush my teeth while staring at her through the bathroom mirror. I was not up for this argument right now.

"Hello, Christopher? Are you just going to keep looking at me or say something?" she asked. I just continued to brush in silence until I was finished.

"Listen Erin, I don't need a lecture from you too," I said while stepping past her and heading towards my bedroom.

"I'm not lecturing you. I just want to know what's up. What two women are not enough for you?" she asked standing directly in front of me. She was pissed.

"I'm not running around chasing after no woman, is you the fuck crazy? Y'all two are more than enough. You are tripping. I'm cool on that aspect," I said trying to step around her as she stepped to the side blocking me. I made a mental note to stop having arguments in the bedroom. Renee does this same shit.

"So, what is it? You're out here running these streets again, Chris? Are you that dumb?" Erin said as she begins to break down "You stupid if that's what you're doing."

"Stop with the water works," I said grabbing her into my arms. I hated this part. I felt bad for her break down.

"Erin," I said kissing her on her lips. "I love you babe, just calm down." I started kissing her again as she returned my passion.

"You worry too much," I told her as I lifted her shirt over her head revealing her 36 D's with pink stiff nipples. I sucked on them one at a time as she cradled the back of my head to her chest.

"I already only have part of you, Chris. I can't imagine having anything less than what I already have now," she said as I kissed her stomach and pulled down her sweatpants and panties.

"I'm not going nowhere," I said to her while looking into her eyes.

She reached for the waistline of my shorts and pulled them down as my penis sprung out at attention. She grabbed it and began stroking me while dropping to her knees. Licking the pre-cum from my slit, she teased me by licking along the underside before engulfing me in her warmth. Her mouth was so wet and the slurping noises only add to the feeling she gave me, which was pleasure.

I knew what we were doing was wrong, but I truly felt for Erin and she sex me better than Renee could ever.

"Shit babe." I moaned as she deep throated me. I loved watching my dick side in and out of her mouth. I grabbed the back of her head as she sucked and slurped sloppily. "Damn, E!" I said while rocking my hips, fucked her mouth and her throat.

She slobbered all over my thick dick as I pulled her face deeper into my groin.

"Mmm!" she mons as she hummed on my meat. I continued to enjoy my dick being sucked while I watched her concentrate on what she was doing. She was passionate about pleasing me and I loved that about her. I craved it. I sped up the thrust of my hips, fucking her face and the only thing that can be heard in the room was the sloppy slurping sounds of her mouth as she let me feed her.

"Get on the bed," I told her as I guided her to lay her on her back.

"No! I want it like this!" Erin said crawling to the center of the bed and putting her ass in the air. "I want you to fuck this pussy and beat it up daddy."

Her talking to me like that turned me on even more. As I got behind her and slid my dick between her thick pussy lips, I entered her, and she pushed back wiggling her ass against me. I grabbed her waist as I started to thrust inside of her. I strongly thrusted trying to bury myself inside her pussy.

"Aah! Yes, fuck!" Erin groaned as her pale phat ass bounced off my pelvis.

"Mmm! Yes Chris! Like that!" She yelled as I fucked her hard and steady. I slapped her ass on both sides making her ass cheek turn beet red.

"Who pussy is this, ma?" I questioned fucking her deeply.

"Yours! Fuck yeah! It's been yours," she moaned as I slapped her again. "Oh shit, yes, yes! Get this pussy, daddy!" she panted, thrusting her ass back against me. I fucked her for all I was worth.

"Chris, I'm coming! Fuck me baby!" she yelled. I felt my nut building and fucked her until I explode. I pumped my load deep inside her pussy before she turned around and sucked the rest out of me. "Damn Erin, what the fuck!" I said as I rode my orgasm.

"I had to clean you off," she said as she laid down beside me. Breathing heavy, I said, "Erin, you're a freak."

"That's what keeps your sexy big dick ass coming back," she countered as we shared a laugh. It fell silent for a moment as I laid there holding her.

"Can I tell you something? And please take it with love, Christopher." she said to me while looking me in my eyes.

"What's up E?" I asked.

"Stay out on the streets, please. We can manage to find a way that doesn't include that. On top of that we need you. I need you, Renee, Zya, Siren–we all need our king, and these little girls need their father."

she said to me.

"I know that already–wait, what!?" I asked, sitting up. "What do you mean father? How can I be Zya's father?" I had hoped this bitch was lying.

"You heard me, Chris!" she yelled to me. This bitch trapped my ass.

"Zya? I'm Zya's father?" I asked, shocked and angry all at once.

"Did you ever look at her Chris? She looks just like you and Siren, plus you can obviously tell she's black," she stated.

"I never thought that though. Shit! Erin, why would you even keep something like that from me?" I asked.

"What difference would it make?" she said to me. There was a huge difference. What would Renee say about this? How could I tell her? She could never find out until I figured shit out.

"A big ass difference," I countered.

"Sorry Christopher, but she's yours. Just please don't get yourself locked up. That's the only reason I'm even giving you this information–you have too much out here to lose.

"Get up!" I said as she just looked at me like she didn't hear me. "Come on! Get the fuck up and get dressed," I snapped.

"You're kicking me out?" Erin asked and I can see the hurt in her eyes, but this was too much for me to handle right now.

"Sorry, but I got to get ready to go and that was unexpected. You just shook me up, so yes, you have to go for now. I'll see you sometime later. If not, call me," I said getting up out of bed and heading into the bathroom, locking the door. What the fuck was she thinking holding that from me? What the fuck am I going to tell Renee?

TRYING TO UNDERSTAND
Adrian

"So tell me why you never bothered to tell me any of this?" I said to Chris as I racked the balls on the pool table. We were on Broad and Dauphin at the pool bar and I couldn't believe what he just said to me.

"Come on Adrian. You're my best friend man, I already knew if I would've told you about what I had going on with Erin you wouldn't let me be. You would've been looking at me the same way you are now," Chris stated while downing another beer.

"That's because you're fucking insane. It's not just some random chick; it's her best friend who she's always around. That's a double edge sword. And not only the sex and affair, but you fathered her daughter, who is damn near the same age as Siren. Man, if Renee ever found out about this, you better pray she doesn't kill you," I said grabbing the pool stick and breaking the rack of balls.

"Tell me something I don't know. I feel bad all the way around the board on this one. I mean I'm seriously fucked up," Christopher said while getting ready to take over after I missed my first shot.

I stepped off to the side, giving him some room. "Yeah, it's a fucked up situation completely," I said, shaking my head at the thought. I asked him, "How does the little girl act around you?" which caused him to miss his shot as well. "You could go again."

"No need, but she just acts like any other regular kid that would act around their friend's parents. But that's bothering me also. You know how many times she has been around Siren and I? You saw how Siren acts around me. I keep playing in my head and wondering how she feels thinking she doesn't have a father. Every little girl loves their father, especially if he's a good one," Christopher said as he ordered another beer.

"You know, you might want to slow down on those drinks. They're not going to take away what you're feeling," I said leaning over to aim at the three ball. "What did Erin tell her about her father then and what's her name again?" I asked.

"Who?" he said, trying to concentrate on making his lucky number go in the pocket.

"Your daughter is the one we're talking about," I said.

"Zya, and do you have to say that like that?" Chris states as he looks around like we'll be overheard.

"Sorry," I said sincerely, "but if everything checks out and this is the truth, then it's your responsibility to fix that emptiness in her life. I'm just curious on how you're going to go about this. Every angle I imagine, I just see a battle ahead of you," I admitted to him as I took a step away from the pool table and over towards the bar.

"I know that Adrian, but you know Renee. Who knows how she is going to react," he said while staring into space. I could tell he had a lot of his mind, and he didn't even know where to begin to express himself.

"At the same time, it's your daughter, man. You can't neglect her no matter what you know. You did one of the worst things possible you could've done to a black woman." I said.

Chris looked at me like he didn't know what he did wrong and said, "What's that?"

I looked at him straight in his eyes and said, "You cheated on her and had a baby with a white girl."

"She might not see it like that. They are best friends," he said, trying to sound hopeful.

"Man try this scene on the black women of this world and I'm sure more than 75% of them are going to see it like that. It's like a slap in the face to their history on earth."

"Shit, I got to do something," Chris said as I checked my phone and replied back to a text from Kelly. Lately, we have been talking a lot. Something about her just interested me.

"Adrian!" Chris said, snapping me out of my phone.

"I'm here with you," I assured him.

"You zoned out on me, man. Like, what am I supposed to do?" he said to me looking like a lost soul trying to find his way back to life. I didn't know what to tell him except man up and deal with it, but Chris was my friend, and I was supposed to help him out.

"No, I was replying back to a text actually," I corrected him. "I really have no idea for you. It's a sensitive situation."

"I know who that is. Isn't she the one from the restaurant you spoke to?" Chris inquired. I nodded my head. "I can't believe you said she's a judge. That's rare—a Black female judge," Chris stated as I took a swig of my drink before I corrected him.

"She's actually white," I said, and the shock on his face was evident.

"I didn't even know you dated white women." he said.

"Come on man, I'm not racist," Chris shot back at me.

"Never said you were."

"It's just in all my time knowing you, I never heard or saw you with one, so I always thought you had a preference." I countered, walking towards the pool table.

"That's a good thing. I guess I'm trying something different. I mean it sounds like she's good to have around."

"Her name is Kelly. And I thought that too, but you know me. I'm not looking for a relationship or anything long term." I told him.

"You kill me with that. So what happens when you really find someone you like everything about?" Chris asked me.

"Don't know. It has hasn't happened yet," I answered honestly.

"Well, it's your life. Just do what you always tell me—keep it simple and just let that be known every step of the way so there's no confusion," Chris quoted me.

"I wish you would have done that. Now I got to worry about planning your funeral every day after what you did. Are you still messing around with Erin?" I questioned and his expression told it all.

"Come on Chris. Man, are you suicidal? Just make sure you tell me your last request."

"Just take care of my daughters, Adrian. She might really try to take me out for this," he told me with fear in his eyes.

Kelly

I was sitting here contemplating if I was going to invite Adrian over to my place. That was his request being as though we already went to his. I was excited at the thought of seeing him again. I hadn't actually seen him in person since we had lunch. I never noticed how much I missed the feeling that comes with being with someone.

"Kelly, are you paying attention to me?" Jerrie asked as we pulled up to the nail salon.

"Yeah, girl why wouldn't I be?" I lied. All I kept thinking about was Adrian and that night. I was so free. Free from everything which made having sex with him exciting and new.

"Uh huh, so what was I talking about?" she asked me. I couldn't help but smile at the fact that she busted me.

"Okay, I'm sorry. I was thinking about something that's all."

"Thinking about what? Is everything okay?" she asked.

I couldn't help but have a huge smile on my face, "Yeah. I just had Adrian on my mind," I admitted.

"Don't be one of those girls, Kelly. Do not be dick whipped and all." She stared at me with a stern look on her face. I can tell she was concerned for me and Adrian, but it was innocent for the most part. I just wanted to enjoy what I had with a man that had no secret agenda.

"Oh lord here we go with the 'Don't tell me one of those girls who loses their shit when they get a new dick' speech," I asked as we got out of the car and headed inside of the salon.

"Yes, you know soon one of those simple-minded chicks that gets a man and starts acting all new on a sister," Jerrie said to me. I heard her loud and clear, but I wasn't like that.

"Come on, Jerrie. I love you girl I will never do that. I'm just enjoying my little chocolate bar for the moment," I said as we sign in with the receptionist and tell her what we would like done. I needed to get a refill and a pedi; I had to keep the girls looking fresh for him. I don't want him to see me slacking.

"So, it was little right? Damn, I hate being wrong. I thought he was the type to have a big, long thing," Jerrie admitted. I couldn't with her sometimes.

"Nope," I said to her as we took a seat to get our pedicures. All this dick talking made me forget what color I wanted. "He's actually big."

"Oh my God, I called it! Like, I really did. Was its good, Kelly?" she asked me. As much I wanted to tell her every detail, I didn't want her eyeing him like a piece of meat when he came around.

"Jerrie, that man had me screaming. I mean I was screaming for Jesus so much Saturday night that I had to go to praise him Sunday morning," I said. As we giggled, the nail tech came over and asked us to choose the color we wanted. Something told me to go with scandalous red so I did.

"I need something like that at home so I can work," Jerrie said, grinding her hips in her chair. "You must really like him, huh?"

"Honestly, I do, but I'm not putting myself out there like that. I'm just playing it for what it's worth for now." I told her as we were called back for our manicure treatment.

"See you after we are both done," I told her as we separated. I loved times like this where I could just pamper myself. Plus, having Adrian come over tonight will be something I would enjoy. I finished getting my nails and toes done, and after waiting for Jerrie to finish paying her bill, Jerrie dropped me back off at home.

"Jerrie, I feel like a hoe," I admitted to her.

"I mean, you did get red polish," she said with a laugh, "but why though?"

"I've just met this man and I gave him all the goodies."

"That's not so bad. I mean I don't think so. You were due to get that kitty scratched," Jerrie said and found amusement in her own words.

"But I feel like he's going to think of me as a hoe for being so easy. I should've made him wait a bit…" I confessed to her.

"Hopefully you didn't go all out girl. Tell me you held back some. I mean you can't fuck a man to crazy on the first night you just met."

"Nothing too crazy, just blindfolded sex, but I don't know where it might go tonight," I continued.

"You seeing him again tonight? You little freak!" she said with a smile on her face. Yes, yes, yes, I was a freak but that didn't change the fact that I fucked him before I even got to know his favorite color.

I blushed. "I like his company. What can I say?"

"Shit, you like more than his company, I can tell you that," Jerrie said while pulling up into my driveway.

"You coming in?" I asked.

"No. Just get ready for your company, little freak. I love you. Call you tomorrow," she said while pulling out of my driveway.

Well, I guess she was right. I might as well go follow orders. I headed into the house and retrieve my cell phone out my purse to make my arrangement final.

BEING EXPOSED
Renee

"Sabrina, what are you doing here?" I asked as I opened my door to find my co-worker standing on my doorstep. I was so irritated at the sight and thought of her being here, especially after getting caught in my bedroom with her.

"I came here to talk. Are you going to let me in or what?" she asked, matching my agitation.

I wanted to say, "Hell fucking naw, we can talk right here just like this." Then I decided against it. I didn't want my nosy ass neighbors to hear or for Chris to pull up seeing her here.

"Come on but make it fast," I said reluctantly. I moved to the side of the door allowing her to pass by me. "What's this about anyway?"

She rolled her eyes as she answered, "Really? Come on, you know what this is about, Renee. Why do you keep avoiding me? What's up with that?"

Of course, I was going to lie to her. I couldn't tell her what had been happening since that night. "Nobody is avoiding you. I've just been busy."

"Busy doing what? We work at the same hospital?" she said while interrupting me. But of course, I wasn't lying. I've been busy trying to make Chris forgive me and keeping my family together. She will never understand the position she put me in since that night. But, on the other hand, who the hell did she think she was? I didn't have to explain shit to her.

"You know what, I'm just going to keep it real with you. Chris saw us in the bedroom last time you we're here, and I panicked because he didn't take it so well. I didn't mean to just give you the cold shoulder or nothing, but I don't know what else to do about it," I said, happy I got it off my chest.

"So, he actually saw us? Why didn't you just say something about it to me? I could've understood that," she said. I felt relieved that she took it so well.

"I didn't know what I was supposed to say? It's over between us. It was fun but my husband was not with it?" I asked.

"No… but is that what you're saying to me?" Sabrina asked. I wondered what the fuck she thought I was saying this whole time.

"Basically," I stated while growing impatient. She shifted her weight to one side.

"So, you just saying fuck our relationship, huh?"

This bitch was crazy because she thought we were going to live happily ever after while I was still married.

"Don't just put this all on me, Sabrina. You knew I had a husband when we started doing what we did. I'm not leaving my husband for no one nor am I risking my marriage and family for that matter," I said snapping my neck. She must have lost her mind.

"So, what we had just meant nothing to you?" she asked, and her hurt was evident in her tone.

"I'm not saying that, but Sabrina, I'm not gay," I stated frankly.

The look of disbelief was written all over her face.

"So, when you were humping your pussy against my face what did you call that? Scratching an itch? Bitch please, you're gay," she spat and I started to smack the shit out of her, but I heard a car pulling up, which I assumed was Christopher. I looked out the window and sure enough, it was Chris pulling into the driveway which sent me into another panic mode as I rushed back over to Sabrina.

"Come on, please hide," I said as I guided her into the dining room.

"I'm not hiding no fucking where that's your husband not mine," she said, protesting where she stood.

"Bitch, please get in the fucking closest or you won't make it out this damn house," I told her while shoving her to the closet with more urgency. My heart was beating a thousand miles per minute, and I was starting to sweat.

"This is some bullshit, Renee," she stared angrily at me like I cared about her feelings. My whole world was about to blow up in my face right now, so I could give two shits about her right now.

"We'll talk about it some other time, I promise. Just not right now," I said closing the closet door and as soon as I do the front door begins to open.

"Mommy!" Siren said, running into the house in front of her dad.

"How was mommy's little angel's day at school today?" I asked squatting down to talk to her after giving her a hug.

"It was good. We made paintings today in class," she said, smiling from ear to ear. Seeing that little girl's face made all my problems vanish. But I still had Sabrina in the closet, and I knew she could hear every single word.

"You did? Where is this painting? Mommy wants to see what her baby made," I said going into her book bag.

"Daddy got it in his car," she said while turning around to the front door.

"He does? You showed daddy before me? I thought we were girl power?" I asked offended but secretly thinking about how I was going to sneak Sabrina out of my house.

"We are silly, but he's my dad," she said, sounding so innocent and adorable. I couldn't even be mad at that answer. I got up and gave my husband a kiss.

"How was your day?" he asked me. Truth be told, it was a shit show. If only he knew what was behind door number two, everything would be exposed.

"I guess you can say it was okay. I didn't do much. I just washed some clothes and paid the cable bill you keep forgetting about," I reminded him.

"Sorry about that," he stated. "I 'll pay you back." Trust me, money was the first thing from my mind.

"No need I used your credit card. I couldn't let Siren go without. You know that girl loves her SpongeBob," I said using his weak spot against him. "But I have something for you too," I admitted. I was desperately trying to get him upstairs without being obvious. My eyes are locked on that closet.

"What's that?" he said while taking a seat on the sofa. *Just please get up,* I said to myself. *I don't need no more bad blood between us.*

"Follow me and I'll show you," I said heading upstairs. "Siren please put your bookbag somewhere that you won't forget. I'm not trying to have another search party like I did this morning." I continued as she looked up at me.

Chris was not too far on my heels and soon we were in our bedroom with him picking me up and placing me on the bed as he kissed me.

"You missed me huh?" he asked.

"Always," I answered, helping him take off his shirt. My juices were flowing, and he was just about to go down on me when Siren came banging on the bedroom door.

"Mommy! I want to play!" she screamed, and Chris got up to unlock the door.

"Shit!" I said out loud, a bit frustrated as she ran up to me.

"Can I play please, Mommy?" she asked, looking at me while sitting up in the bed and kicking her feet.

"We weren't playing anything, angel. Daddy and I were talking," I explained to her, hoping that she didn't open that closet. I didn't need this drama right now.

"No, you and the lady in the closet. I want to play hide and seek too!" My heart dropped to my ass as she spoke those words. The warmth in my body went cold. I couldn't believe that this is happening right now. How can I fix this?

"What!? What did you just say?" Chris asked her, sounding like a crazed man which even scared Siren. He took off down the steps to the closet, as I ran behind him. I was terrified and hoped like hell he wouldn't do something crazy. I hoped her stupid ass wasn't still in this house. He opened the closet with force and stepped in, searching it like a mad man.

"Siren!" he shouted while heading back upstairs. "Where did you see this lady?" he asked her. I couldn't think straight. What was I supposed to say? Who was I supposed to blame?

I could hear everything, but I was paralyzed at the moment. Fear has taken over my body and I was left standing in the living room as I hears Siren's voice.

"She left out the door when I put my bookbag away."

I was thankful but also fearful of what I knew was to come. Christopher spent some time upstairs before coming back down and heading for the front door. I wanted to stop him, but I couldn't. My mind wouldn't let my body move.

Before he left, he stated, "I want a divorce," before closing the door behind him. The moment the door closed, I fell to my knees. My life was over, and I started broke down.

Kelly

The doorbell rang announcing Adrian's arrival and Lola went wild as I put her in the backyard.

"Come on girl please don't act like that," I said while closing the backdoor after putting her out. Lola was my baby, but I was too excited about tonight to pay her any mind. I gave myself a once over again in the mirror before going to the door. "I'll be right there!"

You know a girl can't seem to be excited, I thought as I smoothed out my dress before opening the door.

"Hey beautiful," Adrian said, leaning in giving me a hug and kiss on the cheek. I couldn't help but to inhale whatever fragrance he had on. The man smelled good.

"Glad you could make it," I said as I closed the door behind him.

"It smells good in here; What you cook?" Adrian said, stepping into the living room.

"Something I hope you'll enjoy," I said, playing around as he takes a whiff of the air. "I was also hoping we can talk more face to face. I wanted to see if you can keep that same attitude," I said as he smiled at me and took his jacket off.

"Remember, Kelly. You're not just inviting me over to talk over dinner..."

"You're really into yourself, aren't you?" I asked, feeling as though he was being a bit too cocky for my liking.

"No, I'm really just into you," he said taking a step closer to me. "So now we're face to face like you wanted... tell me, how much do you like me, Kelly?" he asked when grabbing my hand and kissing the back of it before placing it to his cheek then down to his chest.

"I think you're okay, why?" I asked as I felt his muscular chest beneath my hand.

"Just okay?" he asked. He kissed me on my lips and I felt my womanhood come alive between my thighs. "You know your eyes tell another story," he said nibbling on my neck. I had to pull myself away from him.

"Okay, maybe a little more than okay, but I'm not going to help your head get any bigger than what it already is," I said walking into the kitchen. "Are you ready to eat?"

"If you are ready. Can I help you with anything?" Adrian asked, which I found to be a pleasant gesture. Normally men seemed to just love to be waited on. At least the ones I normally dated.

"Sure, but I'm pretty much done quite honestly."

"So, what can I do for you then? I like to feel like I earned my meal," he asked.

"Umm, you can begin by taking your shirt off and continue to look cute," I said with a grin.

"Now that sounds sexy, especially coming from a judge. Is that how you give orders in the courtroom?" he asked, shaking his head.

I laughed at his joke. "I like to think of myself as a fair judge and I do believe in people sometimes. So, you can do this community service or some jail time… your choice."

"Am I on trial?" Adrian asked with a questionable expression on his face.

"Yup. So, what's it going to be? Are you going to give the lady something to look at or what?" I said with a smirk on my face. I couldn't wait to see him naked. His soft skin against his hard muscles. His perfectly round ass. Everything about this man was beautiful.

"I don't believe I have much of a choice," he says, pulling his shirt over his head and revealing his impressive torso.

"You work out I see," I said admiring his body.

"I try to. You got to take care of your body, you know," he said rubbing his abs while looking in my eyes.

"Umm humm," I said, starring. This man looked good, and I just made my mind up. I knew I was climbing this mountain of chocolate tonight.

"Kelly!" He shouted, but I couldn't hear anything he was saying.

"Umm hmm," I replied, still staring at him.

"The food!" he shouted again, still not understanding.

"What about it?" I asked in a daze.

"The food, Kelly!" he said as he was pointing to the pot that was boiling over.

"Oh shit!" I said rushing over to turn down the heat of the stove. "Let me ask you something, Adrian," I said stirring the noodles in the pot.

"Go ahead," he said while cleaning up the water that was on the stove.

"Why is it—no, let me rephrase that. What is it you like about me?" I asked. "I mean that night at OOKA, I didn't say one word to you."

"And?" he stood behind me. I could feel how close he was just by his body heat coming off him and by the way he smelled. The wetness in my panties was starting to grow even more.

I turned around to talk to him to his face. "What made you want to talk to me?" I asked as he leaned on the counter.

"Well, to be honest, besides you being beautiful, it was how calm and reserved you were that made me very interested," he admitted.

"But you said you want someone who's adventurous and wild and that just made me think of Jerrie that night. She just screams 'life of the party' and me–not so much," I told him.

"That's the loud one, right?" he asked while reaching for my hand.

"Yes," I said.

"You know, just because she is more outspoken doesn't mean she is more adventurous. It's willingness. Willingness to try something new and different. Willingness to let go of that calm person and let something else take over, or in your case, someone else. Being blindfolded and giving yourself to me sexually. Have you ever done that before?" Adrian asked.

"No." I confessed. I had only hoped he would do something like that to me again. As he kissed my hand, he said, "Exactly and you enjoyed it, or I wouldn't be here today."

This man made points I would've never ever thought of. Yes, I liked how he blindfolded me. Taking away one of my senses really let me focus on my orgasm much more. I needed to know more about this man.

"Do you like controlling women?" *Why did I just ask that?*

He laughed at my question. Damn, that must have been stupid to ask.

"Dominating women yes, but not just in a S&M type of way. I want the challenge, the energy, and sometimes even the chase," he said while taking a step closer to me.

"That sounds nice to hear coming from the opposite sex. I'm not used to hearing a man admit that honestly," I said looking away from him.

He lifted my chin up with his finger so we could look each other in the eyes.

"It's okay. When I asked 'are you're willing' I was asking you are you willing to be dominated? Are you willing to give control over to me? Are you willing to match my energy?" he said taking a step around the island until he was standing in front of me. I felt so small next to his tall frame.

"When it comes to being nasty and freaky, are you willing to challenge your sexual exploitation?" he asked, staring me in the eyes. I knew we were in the kitchen, but I swear, the heat went up to a thousand degrees.

"It's not just sexual with me either. If we were doing business on any type of level, and you see I'm ambitious and dedicated, can you match my drive and dedication? Will you be willing to put in just as much hard work as me? That even includes relationships. If I'm giving you all of me, can you give me the same?" he said just inches away from my lips.

"Are you asking me?" I said while looking up at him.

"I am," he started looking down at me.

SITUATIONSHIPS
Adrian

"Fuck!" I said slapping Kelly on her ass as I thrusted into her. We had been going at it since dinner.

"Yes, umm yes!" she moaned, gripping the sheets of the bed as I fucked her from behind. Her pussy was good, and I couldn't get enough of her tonight.

I gripped her waist and continued to pound into her. She moaned, arching her back as I squeezed her right cheek and watched my shaft enter her pinkness.

"Make this pussy squeeze this dick while I'll fuck you." I told her reaching and grabbing a fist full of her hair.

"Oh shit, oh shit, oh shit, yes, harder!" she said as I felt her pussy muscles clamp down on my shaft. I thrusted deep inside her, wanting her to know she couldn't deny me. I wanted her to understand that I ran her pussy.

"That's right. Give me this good pussy." I told her as I slapped her on her ass again.

"Adrian baby, I'm coming. I'm coming, baby," Kelly groaned as I long stroked her deep and fast.

"Don't come on this dick yet," I said causing her to groan in protest and frustration. I just continued to fuck her at this pace as she moaned loudly. I knew I was torturing her, and I knew it wouldn't be long before she couldn't help but climax.

"Umm shit," she groaned as her body trembled. I knew she was close. I rubbed her clit faster as I stroked her.

"Don't let me go. Enjoy it, Kelly," I said pounding her pussy. "Are you mine, Kelly? Talk to me," I said. She tried to run away from me, but I grabbed her hips and pulled her back.

"I'm--yours Adrian. Shit, ohh shit, fuck. I can't baby. I'm so— sorry!" she yelled as she squirted all over my dick and thighs before collapsing on her stomach shaking. I crawled on top of her back and planted kisses up her spine until I reached the nape of her neck.

"We're not done yet," I said kissing her lips.

"I can't take no more. She's tired down there," she said.

"So, you're just going to leave me like this?" I asked pointing down at my still erect penis. She smirked before moving from under me as I rolled over on my back. She went down on me.

Now it was my turn to be at her mercy. She bobbed her head up and down on my shaft.

"Shit!" I said placing my hand on top of her head to guide and control her pace. She slurped loudly and I enjoyed the erotic sounds that comes from her mouth.

She moaned around my shaft and the vibration brought even more sensation to my body. I looked down to watch her; she was on her knees in the bed playing with her clit as she worked her tongue around the tip of my penis.

She seemed to be enjoying herself and she was doing a hell of a job. I felt my balls start to tighten as I reached my point of no return.

"I'm about to nut," I told her and she just lowered her mouth all the way down to the base, taking my penis into her throat.

"Shit! Oh shit, Kelly, damn!" I said as I tried to move away from her.

I didn't know how to explain what she was doing to me, but it felt like she was fucking me with her throat and the sensation was causing my body to jerk uncontrollably as my sperm squirted down her throat. "Fuck, fuck, fuck!" I said as my body spasmed with every squirt. Kelly kept on sucking me without skipping a beat as she swallowed everything I had to give until I was too sensitive to endure anymore.

She looked up and stared at me with a mischievous grin on her face.

"You think that's funny, huh?" I asked as she crawled up beside me.

"You started this," she countered pressing her body into my own. "Honestly, I'm glad I did," I admitted. "That was great."

"Sure was," she agreed. "Oh my, look what time it is. I didn't know it got so late." I followed her line of sight and saw the clock said 1:12 am.

"I didn't mean to keep you up so late. I know you have court tomorrow, right?"

"Monday through Friday," she stated.

"I think I should get ready to go then." I tried to get up but she stopped me.

"Don't go yet. I want to talk for a while," she said with a yawn.

Something in me told me I should go but I stayed and granted her request.

"So, what would you like to talk about, Ms. Patten?" I asked.

"Please don't call me that. That sounds so old and reminds me of my mother," she said, smiling with her eyes close. "Could you tell me the real reason why you're still single?" The question hit me by surprise; I pondered it for a minute and then finally let my guard down.

"I'm honestly afraid of being hurt and let down by someone that close to me," I admitted.

"Something happened?" Kelly inquired.

"Life happened," I stated flatly. "It's just some people use the word love too loosely. Some confuse caring and loving someone with infatuation with someone. It's two different meanings completely, some even say three. I just try my best to be careful where I place my heart," I said. I waited for her response, but she didn't answer. She was sound asleep on my chest. I just laid there holding her until she soon closed her eyes and I soon followed after her.

Christopher

I haven't been home in a couple of days, let alone on my block. I meant what I said when I left that house, I wanted a divorce. I had enough of the disrespect from her. I looked past her affair with the chick the first time but to have that bitch back inside my house again with my child there to witness it was the straw that broke the camel's back.

I wouldn't even be on this block if it wasn't for what I needed to do with Erin and Zya, I thought to myself. I looked down at the Rite-Aid bag in my hand which had the home paternity kit so I could be sure that she was my daughter. I believed Erin, but with what's going on with me and Renee I started to question a lot when it came to women.

I rang the bell to Erin's house thinking to myself that maybe I should have called before I just came over here like this.

"Who is it?" I heard her call out from the other side of the door.

"Chris," I stated before she opened the door.

"What's going on with you? Is everything okay?" she asked, peaking out the door.

"Everything is fine. I just needed to talk to you for a minute. Do you mind?" I asked. She looked me up and down before letting me in.

"Like for real, are you alright, Chris?" she asked as she closed the door behind me. I took a seat on the couch.

"All depends on what's your definition of alright?" I said lying down on her couch, thinking about my predicament. "Physically I'm alright, mentally and emotionally not so much," I admitted as she sat on the edge of the couch rubbing my chest.

"Is this something to do with why you haven't been home in the last couple of days?" she asked me while she rubbed my back.

"Yeah, and I see you been talking to Renee." I was annoyed at the thought of her. "Did she tell you everything?"

"No, and I didn't ask. I don't pry into y'all's marriage, you know that," she said.

"Well, let me ask you something then..." I turned and looked at her. "Did you know your best friend was into women?" I asked looking at her for any indication. I wondered if I was the only one left in the dark.

"Renee? Hell no. She never mentioned or indicated that to me and you know how long me and Renee have known each other. Is she a lesbian? Hold on, wait she can't be that. She's married to you. Is she bi-sexual?" Erin asked with an expression of disbelief. I remained silent, stuck in my thoughts. So it wasn't just me my wife had been deceiving this whole time.

"Chris snap out of it. I'm sorry to hear that, but don't stop going home. Think about Siren."

I thought about what Erin had to say. "It doesn't change the fact that I wanted a divorce," I stated flatly as Erin stopped rubbing my chest.

"I never heard you talk like that before." she stated.

"That's because I never felt how I feel now. I need to be loved." I said grabbing her hand and pulling her on top of me, I kissed her lips. I needed her. I needed the way she made me feel. I knew she could love me.

"What's in the bag?" Erin asked, catching me off guard. I hesitated for a second not wanting another argument.

"It's something for Zya..." I said as she looked in the bag.

"What the fuck is this, Chris?" she asked, looking at it with anger in her eyes.

"It's a home paternity test for me and Zya." I told her.

"So, what the fuck? You don't believe me when I tell you that's your daughter? So now I'm just some hoe ass bitch out here on the street huh, Christopher?" I could tell her temper was rising.

"Listen, I'm not saying that about you at all, Erin. It's just my head a little mess up from what I'm going through with Renee. I just wanted to be sure."

"So, you mean to tell me because you're going through something with that bitch and her gay ass ways, you're questioning whether I would try to pin a baby on you?" she yelled.

"No, it's not like that."

"It's exactly like that." she screamed over top of me as I got up and tried to calm her down. I reach for her, but she took a step back.

"Don't touch me. You don't love me, Christopher," she said, starting to cry.

"I do love you E. You're tripping."

"So why--why put me and mine through this. I was loyal to you. For years!" she emphasized. "That doesn't mean nothing to you? I'm betraying my best friend for you because I love you! Do you get that?! *I love you.* There hasn't been another man in my bed for years–more than a half a decade. You know how it feels to love someone that fucking much and just watch them give everything you dream of to someone else? My daughter–I'm sorry – our daughter can't even claim her own father because I don't want to cause your world to go upside down." She sobbed and I quickly wrapped my arms around her, trying to console her.

"I love you Erin, I'm sorry. Stop crying, please. I didn't mean it like that. I just wanted documentation, that's it. I want to be a father to Zya and I want to be a better man for you," I told her as I wiped her tears. "Please stop crying."

"You're just saying that now because you're mad at Renee. After y'all kiss and make up, then what? I'll just be left in the same predicament."

"I'm telling you, it's different. You got to trust me, babe." I said, giving her a kiss. She didn't kiss me back.

"I love you, Erin. I just need for you to love me back." This time she was receptive and kissed me back.

I kissed her with a passion and needed her to feel my love and everything I felt for her.

"I need you to trust me," I told her between kisses before I lift her shirt over her head exposing her beautiful breasts and make love to her because she needed it. Shit, I did too.

ACCEPTING CHANGE
Christopher

I didn't want to, but I went against my own stubborn ways and went home after listening to Erin. She was right and made a great point. I couldn't abandon Siren. She was my princess, and she didn't deserve her father neglecting her due to how he felt about her mother.

In last few days since I returned home, Renee and I didn't speak much. She tried to talk to me about what was happening on a few occasions, but I didn't want to hear any of it and let her know it as soon as she started talking about it.

I mean it was self-explanatory in my book. *If a picture is worth a thousand words, seeing something live in action must be worth a best-selling novel,* I thought to myself. Right now, I just wanted to spend some quality time with my daughters. It was a nice day outside, so I called Erin and asked if she and Zya were up for taking a trip to the park today with me and Siren. The girls were enjoying themselves as I watched them try to push each other on the swing.

"You're really quiet. What's going on in your head?" Erin asked, snapping my attention away from the girls. She was sitting right next to me up under the shade of the tree. Ever since I found out the news about Zya being my daughter, I couldn't help but look at the two of them and notice the similarities. I wondered if all parents do that to their children–compare.

"I was actually thinking about my life," I admitted, "but also wondering about the girls. have you ever just looked at the girls and compared their features?"

"For years, I did. It's shocking how much they resemble one another, isn't it?" Erin said.

"Yeah, I was just wondering if I was bugging out for thinking so. Zya and Siren look just alike–Zya just the lighter of the two," I noted. I still had to break the news to Renee. As much as I wanted to hurt her as much as she hurt me, I still loved her because she was the mother of my child.

"Yeah, but their personalities are different. Siren is more outgoing and Zya is more timid," Erin told me, which made me wonder how long she had been observing the two. "They already love each other. I'll tell you that much, and they don't even know they're sisters. I couldn't imagine what their bond would turn into with them knowing."

"I haven't even thought of it like that," I said as I wondered how they would feel.

"What about you, though? How's everything going in the house?" she asked like she didn't already know.

"It's going I guess you can say."

"So that means y'all still not talking to one another?"

"Correct," I told her while still looking at the girls.

"Listen I'm not going to sit here and lie like I don't entertain the thought of us being together one hundred percent, but I don't want you to feel like or even think that I'm swaying you to choose to leave what you already have," she said, leaning her head on my shoulder.

I took in what she said and thought about the state of my marriage and the relationship Erin and I have. I still loved Renee, but our marriage was crumbling and my admiration for Erin kept growing.

"You're not doing anything wrong, Erin so there's no need for you to even think the way you are right now. I meant what I said when I told you about how I'm feeling. I love you, Erin. You have been nothing but good to me and have sacrificed a lot due to the circumstances. That says a lot to me, especially going through what I am now," I told her as I watched the girls run to the slide.

I appreciated the fact that Erin cared so much about everything going on in my life, even though it was with another woman.

"You know, I've been thinking about what you said and if the paternity test will help you get peace of mind, then I'm okay with going through that with you," she told me, which made me snap out of my thoughts. Something about Erin gave me peace of mind and I needed that right now.

"What made you change your mind?"

"You know after my hot-headed self calmed down and started to think about it, I couldn't help but to understand where you were coming from. It's your right to be sure of something like this and I can't deny you of your right of something that's yours, especially if I know a thousand percent Zya is your daughter," she stated and I was relieved she saw it from my point of view. I just wanted to get this behind me.

I mean, I believed her without the paternity test but sometimes you never know.

"Thanks," I said as Mr. Soffee's ice cream truck came pulling up and all the kids went running.

"Dad! Dad! Can we get some ice cream?" Siren asked.

"Is that what y'all want?" I asked getting up and brushing myself off as the two of them nodded their heads enthusiastically.

"They're so cute," Erin said.

"I hope you know one day that's going to be a problem," I said grabbing their hands and heading towards the ice cream truck. "Do you two know what kind of ice cream y'all want?"

"Vanilla," Siren said, jumping up and down.

"I want chocolate with jimmies!" Zya said, swinging back and forth as I held her up.

"Hey, I want jimmies too!" Siren said tugging my other hand.

"It's okay y'all can get whatever y'all want." I said as we approached the truck. We quickly got our cones and went back to our tree.

"Dad, why doesn't Zya have a dad?" Siren asked. It threw me off guard so much that I almost dropped my own ice cream. I looked at Erin for help, but she just looked at me wide-eyed like she was horrified. I turned my attention back to Siren who stood in front of me waiting for an answer.

"Well, who said she doesn't have a dad?" I asked Siren as Zya sat there eating her ice cream.

"She said she doesn't know if she does," she kindly explained it to me.

"Everyone has a dad. Come here, Zya." I called her over and she stood beside Siren.

"You want a dad?" I asked as she nodded. "I'll be your dad; would you like me to be your dad, Zya?"

With no hesitation, she yelled at the top of her lungs, "Yeah!" with the biggest smile on her face.

"Okay from now on how about this, I'll be your dad," I told her.

"What about me?" Siren pouted.

"I'm still your dad too. You don't want to share your dad with Zya?" I can be both of you girl's dad." Siren looked at me like she was trying to comprehend what was going on.

"So that means we're sisters now?" Siren asked while looking at Zya with a smile on her face. "Zya you're my sister now!" Zya smiled back at her and they ran off to continue playing.

"Watch that ice cream!" Erin shouted after them.

I wished things were that simple with the rest of the world, or maybe just mine.

"Those two girls are crazy, but that was a nice way to handle that question. To be honest I always thought about the day Zya would come to me and ask me about her father. I'm happy you were here with me when it happened. I know it's not the formal introduction but for now, I like how they handled it. I was terrified when Siren asked that question," Erin admitted to me.

"You weren't the only one, but I'd rather them go through life for now thinking of each other that way. I mean at least they're together. I would rather them be together than apart," I said while looking at the girls playing. When I finally looked back at Erin, she was just staring at me. "What's your problem?"

"Nothing. I just love you, Chris. You're an amazing man."

Kelly

"Mr. Warfield, by the power invested in me by the state of Pennsylvania, I hereby sentence you to the minimum of eleven and half months to no later than twenty-three months of confinement in Montgomery County Correctional Facility. All court fines and fees will be paid by the defendant, Mr. Fajri Warfield along with restitution for any damage caused by the defendant or incident to the crime committed. Do you understand what I just said, Mr. Warfield?" I asked looking down over to the defendant for confirmation.

"Yes, your honor," he said to me.

"Is there anything you would like to say at this time in open court?" I asked him to give him the courtesy.

"No, your honor," he stated.

"Well Mr. Warfield I hope you straighten up while serving your sentence," I said to him before turning my attention to the people of the court. "Well ladies and gentlemen of the court, the court is now adjourned." I slammed my gavel down and returned to my chambers. That was my last case for the day, and I was happy to be done. I hung my robe and took a seat at my desk. I still had a lot of paperwork to do today; the pile of paperwork and manila envelopes that was sitting on my desk looked kind of intimidating, as though I had to get through it before I could call it a night.

People think this job is easy but having so many people's lives in my hands is a big task to take on. Don't get me wrong–I also knew some judges who didn't care one way or another what happened to an individual, but that wasn't me. Being impartial to me doesn't translate into having a lack of understanding.

I reached for my cellphone to check to see if Adrian texts me and I did. What a nice way to start your load of paperwork – having a man on your mind. His text made me smile for some odd reason. I found myself enjoying him more and more.

Adrian [1:41]

Do you think you'll be able to take a short vacation with me sometime soon?

I didn't know what this man had in mind, but a vacation sounded nice to me.

Me [2:51]

That sounds nice and I have some vacation time but how soon are we talking?

Adrian [2:53]

Like a week or two. Will that be an issue for you?

Me [2:54]

Honestly, I'll have to check my schedule and get back with you on that.

Adrian [2:55]

Well, please keep me in mind.

I started to write him back but decided against it. There was no way I was going to be able to keep the conversation going and still be able to finish reviewing these briefs and motions.

Knock, knock, knock.

"Yes?" I looked up saw my clerk, Megan, entering with more documentation in her hand.

"This just came off the fax for you," she said, handing me what appeared to be a memo sent down from The Supreme Court of Pennsylvania. "I see you have a lot to do here," she said viewing my desk and the paperwork that sits on top of it.

"Tell me about it. I was just about to call or email you anyway. Can you please let me know what my next two weeks schedule looks like or give me a printout of it for my courtroom?" I asked her to read over the news memo I just received.

"Sure, I can do that. Is there anyway else I can help you for the day?" she asked me.

"You can take over and do my job if you like," I said as we both shared a laugh.

"They don't pay me enough to do that much work." Megan said.

"Trust me, I know. Me neither, but please can you let me know the schedule. I'm going to be here past hours with this much paperwork to do, so there's no need to rush." I told her hoping that I could get done in enough time.

"Okay, just take it easy and relax. If you need me, just let me know," she said with a smile before exiting my chambers, closing the door behind her.

"Let's get started," I said to myself as I grabbed the first manila envelope off my desk. It was going to be a long night.

LISTEN TO ME
Adrian

"Wow," Kelly said out of breath as she laid against my chest. "That was amazing." We were watching the sunset after an intense love making session that was outdoors. "I feel so liberated right now," Kelly panted wiggling herself against me.

"Being naked outdoors has a way of making people feel like that," I whispered into her ear as I reached around her to hold her close to me. I never felt that way about a woman before. I could get used to this.

"I still can't believe you have friends that will lend you their entire house when you come out here," she said to me while looking up at me with love in her eyes... or was it lust?

"What can I say? I'm a good guy from the area," I said modestly as I enjoyed the breeze against my flesh coming from the waves of the ocean. I loved the high that I had right now.

"Do you ever think about coming back out here to the west coast?"

Kelly asked. As much as I did, I couldn't leave everything I had built behind. I couldn't tell her that.

"Sometimes," I told her. "I bet there's nicer real estate out here than in Pennsylvania, especially judging by what I have seen so far. I mean that will be great."

"Maybe, but there's a lot more competitors also. I'm not greedy and I enjoyed the lifestyle I have. I mean, I'm not doing bad judging by the hot judge laying against me at the moment," I said, which caused her to turn around and face me.

"Can I be honest with you about something?" she said looking up at me.

"Sure." I kissed her forehead.

"I'm really starting to fall in love with you," Kelly said staring in my eyes. She waited for a reaction, and I held my composure, but honestly, I was dreading hearing those words. I mean, I liked what we had but a relationship was something I didn't see for myself at the moment. "What makes you say that, or think it at least?" I asked her.

I hope she was not saying it because of the vibe we were in now. A lot of people say they love someone either during sex or after but doesn't mean shit.

"I don't think. I actually feel that way about you. I'm not telling you hoping you would profess your feelings for me. I just wanted to share what I was feeling." I think what she meant to say was she loved the sex we had. I mean, I was fine with that because I was good with what we have to.

"I could understand that," I said while holding her tightly as she laid her head on my chest. We were on a reclining deck chair outside on the lawn in the backyard. It was a great moment, and I didn't want to spoil it by coming off cold and distant. I did feel something for Kelly though. Shit, this was the deepest my feelings ever went for any woman.

Come on, Adrian, I thought to myself. I was supposed to be here taking care of business and enjoying my home state of California, but all the emotional talk messed with my frame of mind.

"Come on let's go inside," I said. As the sun finally set, Kelly headed into the house to the master suite as I gathered our clothes and followed. I was going to miss Laguna Beach, but I was ready to get back to the east coast to handle some business.

I truly wished I could shake what I was accustomed to when it came to relationships, but it was what got me to where I was today. I looked at her and I could tell she was disappointed by my response.

"Kelly." She turned to look at me from the side of the bed. "Come here." I said. She walked over stood right in front of me.

"Listen, I'm not used to expressing my emotions and I know that, but I don't want you to think that I don't feel nothing for you because that is far from the truth. I honestly just don't know how to describe what I'm actually feeling for you," I tried my best to get her to understand my standpoint.

"It's okay, Adrian. I told you, it wasn't about what you felt for me. I just wanted you to know how I felt for you because I don't want it to be a surprise to you. I'm falling for you, so if I'm wasting my time, I want you to be straight forward and tell me so. I'm a big girl and I can handle it–good or bad," she said standing in front of me looking me into my eyes.

I laid her back and kissed her passionately. I felt as though she was challenging me, pushing me to confess something I refuse to. I couldn't voice what I wanted to say to her. Something in my mind wouldn't let my mouth say what my heart felt.

"Talk to me Adrian," Kelly said as I kissed on her neck.

"I am talking to you. You're just not listening." I placed my manhood at her opening and entered her slowly. I couldn't form the words to tell her how I felt about her, but I knew damn well I could show her, and that's exactly what I did.

Renee

It was my day off and I felt so relieved because I wasn't feeling too good. I felt like I was coming down with something, so I tried to clean the house from top to bottom. With me being sick, I was trying to eliminate Siren from coming down with the same thing. I was on my hands and knees at the very moment, scrubbing around the downstairs bathroom toilet. In a way, that was my form of peace. Ever since Sabrina showed up at my front door that day, my household had been flipped upside down. Christopher wouldn't talk to me or engage in a genuine conversation unless I initiated it.

I felt as though I was on the verge of losing my marriage for real and the crazy thing about it all was, I wasn't even doing anything foul with Sabrina at that very moment. I was actually trying to cut things off and move forward with my life, but Chris didn't want to hear any of it.

"Stop all that damn running and jumping in there, Siren, you know I don't play that in my house. You're not the hell outside!" I shouted as I heard her heavy thumping coming from the living room came to a stop. She was another one I had a bone to pick with. I knew I couldn't truly be mad at my child for getting me busted, but I didn't have the time nor energy for her shit at the moment.

I continued cleaning the bathroom, when suddenly the smell of the chemicals made my stomach uneasy, which made me gag and vomit into the toilet. *This just hasn't been my month,* I thought as I got up to go upstairs to my bedroom. I needed to lay down. It felt like my body was giving up on me. When I made it to my bedroom and laid down, I thought about how things got to this point, but soon enough, I was sound asleep.

"Renee, wake the fuck up!" Christopher shouted, shaking me as he stood over me like he's possessed or something. I might had been disoriented, but Chris' anger was evident. I quickly woke up and panicked wondering if he finally snapped. "What the hell are you doing?! You don't smell that?! Your daughter was about to burn down the fucking house!" he barked at me and instinctively I jumped out the bed in search of my child.

"Where's Siren?" I asked, heading down the steps, "Siren!" I shouted.

"Yes!" I heard her small voice call out from upstairs. I stopped in my tracks and while standing on the steps I could smell the scent of something burning or at least was burning.

"She's fine, but who knows what would've happened if I didn't make it home on time, Renee? Why did you just leave her unattended like that? What's going on with you?" Christopher asked, looking at me like he wanted to kill me.

I honestly only intended to lay down for a moment. "I was feeling nauseated. I didn't mean to go to sleep Chris." I pleaded with him. It was rare for Chris to get angry like that and I knew he was ready to put his hands on me for endangering his child.

"It doesn't matter what you meant to do Renee, all that matters is what you did and what it could have possibly led to."

"What happened anyway?" I asked, wanting to know the reason why I was getting cursed out.

"The toaster caught on fire. Your daughter called herself making toast because she was hungry, and you were up here sleeping."

"Siren! Get your narrow ass in here!" I called and she took longer than needed to appear. "I know you heard me. Don't make me call you again!" I stated and I saw her little body appear coming down the steps. I just watched her take her sweet time coming down and when she reached the living room, I asked. "What did you call yourself doing?"

She tried to avoid my gaze. "I was trying to make peanut butter and jelly like you make it." I wanted to whip her ass because she knew better.

I guess my expression gave my thoughts away because before I could say something Christopher started, "Don't be mad at her, Renee it's your fault. You should've been keeping an eye on her." When he said that, I totally lost it.

"Don't keep fucking chastising me about my fucking daughter. Alright, I fell asleep and took a nap. My body was tired. She still knows better than to be in the kitchen touching stuff we don't allow her to touch when we awake," I shouted as Chris looked at me like I was crazy. Siren headed back over to the steps.

"Renee, you this close to making me put my hands on you."

"Try it and see how fast you'll be in jail," I retorted. As we stood and stared at each other down, neither one of us wanted to give up our position. I knew I was in the wrong for what could have happened, but a tired parent deserves a nap. Siren was six years old and knew better. Was this all about her knowing right from wrong? No, it was deeper than that. "Listen you don't have to act like this is all this is about Chris. I know you feel like you hate me, and I get that, but when it comes to our daughter, don't question my parenting. I'm sick, and my body needs rest."

"You know what Renee, you absolutely right. It is deeper than this. I'm just tired. I'm tired of feeling like a stranger in my own home all because my so-called wife doesn't know how to keep her legs closed. It's not just men I have to worry about, but women. Women sneaking out of our goddamn house while my daughter is here," he said passionately. As much as I wanted to tell him what really happened that night, I knew he wasn't going to listen. All I could do right now is listen to him and plead my side of things.

"I've tried to tell you numerous times that it isn't like that and that she showed up unannounced to talk and I was trying to cut things off with her. Nothing more," I said starting to feel fatigue.

"Sure, you're right. That explains it all. Y'all was talking and cutting things off and you felt so guilty about quitting things with each other that when you heard me coming, you decided to hide her in the closet and lure me upstairs so she can sneak out the door. Tell me how the hell that sounds?" The way he put it, it did sound bad and ironically, it was the truth.

"That's the truth," I said honestly.

"Right. Like I said before, Renee. Let's call a spade a spade. This is a failed marriage."

"I didn't fail shit and if it's that easy for you to want to call it quits with what we built then how can you say you loved me the way you claim you did?" I asked, feeling my emotions peaking. "Are you serious? You can't be serious…"

He looked at me before he turned to Siren. "Siren get your coat."

"Where are y'all going?" I asked not wanting them to leave, but not wanting to break down in front of them.

"Just out for some fresh air. You said you were tired, so get all the rest you need. I got Siren, so everything's fine. We'll just see you in a few hours," he said, helping Siren into her jacket. I knew I messed up, but I never could have imagined Christopher hating me on this level. I watched as they walked out the front door and took a seat on the couch as my tears started to fall. I was lost. I wanted my marriage back but had no clue on where to start.

BACKSTABBING ME
Renee

My moans and groans echoed throughout the bathroom as I vomited into the toilet. I woke up this morning with my stomach feeling so uneasy. I knew I needed to go get checked out because it just felt like my symptoms were getting worse. I mean, I hadn't felt this bad since... then it hit me. My body hadn't felt like this since I was last pregnant with Siren.

"Oh my God, I can't be..." I said to myself as I tried to think back to my last period. With everything that had been going on in my life lately, I haven't even been thinking nor keeping up with my menstrual cycle.

"Oh my God!" I stated once again, picking myself up from the bathroom floor. I turned on the faucet and stared at myself in the mirror. I looked like a mess, so I splash some water in my face and tried to get myself prepared for today. I was running late for work because I overslept and I blamed Christopher for that. I mean just because we weren't on good terms or even speaking terms, didn't mean he couldn't still wake me up before he took Siren to school.

I hurried and rushed to get dressed and ready to head out to work. It was a nice day outside and I wish I could find some time to enjoy it, but I was in such a rush that I didn't believe that could be possible. Not to mention I needed to stop by a pharmacy to grab a pregnancy test on my way to work. While getting into my car, I thought about what a new baby in the house could possibly mean if it turned out I was indeed pregnant.

At that moment, I was hoping I was wrong; I didn't have my life and household together, and I couldn't handle another major responsibility. I pulled up into the Rite-Aid parking lot on Broad and Susquehanna and quickly ran in to buy a First Response home pregnancy test. My heartbeat was faster with every step after another. As I paid for everything, all I could do is think about how I would tell Chris. Would he believe the baby is his? Could we ever move on with another baby? Will he think I tried to trap him in our marriage with another baby?

When I finally made it to work, I hurried to clock in before going to use the restroom. As I took the stick out of the package, my heartbeat went into overdrive, and I felt myself getting little headed.

"Come on, Renee," I told myself as I squatted over the toilet. So many thoughts wander my mind as I peed on the stick. How would Christopher take to me being pregnant? I remembered how happy he was when we found out about Siren. That made me smile as I waited for the results that could change everything. I glanced at the digital screen of the pregnancy test, and it read: positive. I was indeed with a child. I already assumed I was, but to actually have the confirmation rocked my world.

I took a seat on the toilet and let my reality set in. I was supposed to be happy, but instead, I felt so lost and alone. I was a wife and a mother, but I felt like a tramp and that no one wanted. What the fuck was I supposed to do?

I sat there for a moment gathering my thoughts and putting my game face on because I still had a job to do today and I couldn't let these people see me vulnerable right now.

"Come on Renee. Pull it together, girl." I washed my hands and wiped the tears from my eyes. I wrapped the test in some tissue and put it in my purse before I gave myself the once over in the mirror, making sure I looked okay.

As I made my way to my workstation, I saw my co-worker, Tanya, and greeted her with the best pleasant smile I could muster.

"Hey Tanya," I said with a smile on my face and cheer in my voice.

"How are you, Renee? Is everything okay? I see you running a little late?" she questioned me.

"Yeah, just overslept a little. Did you cover for me?" I asked with a concerned looked on my face.

"You know I at least tried to, but you know that supervisor of ours came around like always and she definitely asked about you," Tanya informed me, and I knew for sure I was busted.

I knew after our last meeting, which didn't end too well, that this would probably lead to another write up. I swear it just felt like things couldn't get any worse for me.

"Thanks anyway, Tanya. I know you, so I know you really tried. You never let me down before," I told her as I started setting my side of the station to my liking. While I got comfortable, I saw my supervisor walking down the hallway towards my direction. I tried to act busy, avoiding eye contact with her, but that didn't work as she appeared directly in front of me.

"Excuse me, Renee. Can I have a word with you in my office?" she asked and reluctantly I walked with her down to her office. As we entered the room, she turned to talk to me.

"For one, how are you doing today Renee?" She looked me up and down which made me feel uncomfortable because I felt like shit.

"I'm doing fine, Sabrina. What's up?" I asked trying to get right to the point.

"Well to be straightforward with you, Renee this is about your attendance," she said.

"Come on, Sabrina. Give me a break, please. I know I was late this morning, but I'm really going through something and I'm sorry. It won't happen again," I said, hoping she would just give me another small reprimand.

"Sorry Renee, but this is over my head and I can't do anything about this one," she told me, which I know is a lie.

"So, what? Am I suspended?" I asked her.

"It's bigger than that, Renee. I'm sorry, but I got to let you go." My world came crashing down on me.

"You got to be kidding me. Is this really how you play?" I asked in disbelief and disgust. I couldn't believe this bitch.

"It's not me, Renee," she said lying through her teeth.

I yell, "Whatever" before walking towards my workstation to gather my things. I couldn't believe my luck.

"Renee!" Sabrina called after me. I continued to ignore her as she followed behind me." Renee, I'm telling you it's not me on this."

I grabbed my purse and jacket.

"Bitch, stop lying! Just be a real bitch and say it! You don't have to pretend with me like you do with everyone else!" I said loudly. My emotions got the best of me as staff and residents stared at the two of us.

"Go ahead, Sabrina. Tell everyone how you just fired me because I won't let you eat my pussy anymore! Tell them!" I shouted as I turned to the crowd. "Hello Everyone! This is my supervisor. She showed up at my house last week and I told her we couldn't continue our affair because I am married and love dick too much to quit it. So, she just fired me because I wouldn't let her taste what's between my legs anymore. This is what Jefferson Hospital represents," I stated before leaving her there with a crowd of onlookers.

"Excuse me!" I said, entering the elevator. "Oh, and Sabrina!" I called, getting here attention. "Fuck you!"

THE TRUTH COMING OUT
Christopher

I pulled up into my driveway in my 2019 Jaguar E-Pace after dropping Siren off at school. I figured I had a moment to enjoy some peace and quiet before I had to meet Adrian so we could go tie up of some loose ends. I figured I might as well get everything ready before I actually had to go, especially while Renee was at work.

I ran in the house and headed to the basement to retrieve the duffle bag he left me containing the product I was supposed to take my cousin, Matthew. I unzipped the bag to check the contents to make sure everything was still there. Before I closed the bag back and took it to my car, I was happy about the timing because if Renee discovered I was back in the street, she would make me a new asshole.

As I stepped away from the car to head back into the house, I noticed Erin heading in my direction, but waited for her back inside. This was the part I hated about our relationship–the secrets, the avoiding of our nosy neighbors–and I told her to come in. Erin looked good in her white blouse and khaki dress pants as she stepped in the house and closed the door behind her.

"You look good," I told her looking at her from head to toe. "You going somewhere?" I asked.

"Actually, yes. I have an appointment scheduled with one of my clients, but that's not for a few hours," she stated as I took a seat on the couch.

"So, what's the surprise visit all about this morning?" I asked all while admiring the shape of her body.

"Damn that hurts. I thought you liked my company."

I smirked. "I do. I like way more than your company..." I told her, but all I kept wondering was what she was up to.

"You play too much. You need to keep your head out the gutter," she said sitting next to me.

"That's nowhere near where I want to put my head at this moment." I leaned over to place a kiss on her neck. She accepted my advances for a moment and suddenly pulled away.

"Hold on that's not why I'm here Chris. Look at you, about to get me all sidetracked," she said while grabbed an envelope from her back pocket.

"What's that?" I asked.

"Just some mail I got today for you." She passed me the folded-up envelope. I honestly didn't know what type of games she was playing until I unfolded the envelope and saw who it was from.

"So, this is it huh?" I asked looking over at her.

"Everything you wanted to know, yes," she said.

"Why didn't you open it?"

"I don't need an someone telling me who I let inside of me." She stated defiantly as I just nodded my head in agreement with her logic.

"You're right, but let's get this over with." I said as I opened the envelope and took out the sheet of paper. I was nervous and excited all at once as I start to read:

"When it comes to the DNA compatibility of Christopher Collins and Zya Collins...wait, Zya last name is Collins?" I was shocked by that information. Erin just looked at me and nodded her head with confirmation.

"Wow... well it reads when it comes to the DNA compatibility of Christopher Collins and Zya Collins, the DNA is 99.999% compatible."

"Meaning she's your blood. Your offspring, your daughter, Christopher," Erin said to me as I stared at the paper in my hand. I couldn't believe she really was my daughter and that Erin let me miss out on so much of her life.

"Chris... hello, Christopher," Erin called to me. It took me a moment to get it together, but I did.

"My bad, I just was in my head." I confessed to her.

"Thinking about what? I know this is a lot to handle," she said.

"Thinking about all the times I missed with Zya. I feel cheated in a way." It's a lot to handle. I don't think any man can handle finding out that they have another child in this world, let alone right next door.

"What exactly did you miss, Christopher? You were at every birthday party. You actually helped pay for them. You live right on the same block, and you picked Siren and Zya up from the same school. I even messed up your back seat when my water broke, remember?" she asked while laughing at herself.

She moved closer to me, "You were around her whole life, and even though you didn't know you were her father, you treated her still with tender love and care."

"I just don't want my daughter to be a secret," I admitted.

"She doesn't have to be. I know what type of man you are and I'm with you regardless, but if that's what you want to do, scream it for all I care. Take pride in what we made. That's our beautiful little girl who would love to be able to show off her father," she said. I knew she was right. I took in everything she said and appreciated everything she did for me so far. She really was supportive and sacrificed a lot when it came to me.

"I love you Erin, and honestly, I believe I'm in love with you," I said as I placed the envelope and letter on the table.

"I'm in love with you too, but what made you say that just now." she asked me.

"It's how I feel," I said leaning over to kiss her lips. She returned it, matching my passion.

"How much time do you have until you need to see your client?" I asked.

"I have a couple hours. Why do you ask?"

"You know why I asked." I grabbed her, placing her short self on my lap and started to kiss her again. I held her close as I suck on her bottom lip and unbuttoned her blouse.

"Chris, you drive me crazy," she said as carried her upstairs. I wanted to be comfortable and able to take my time pleasing her.

When I reached my bedroom, I laid her down on the bed and removed her bra before unbuttoning her pants, exposing her beautiful vagina. Once they were off, I took my time kissing my way up her thick thighs until I reached her sweet spot and when me and her lips met, I placed a kiss on that too.

First, I softly pecked her and then I sucked one lip at a time. She let out a sigh, and I ate her whole, engulfing her as I sucked on her whole womanhood.

"Mmm, that feels good," She breathed as I ran my tongue inside of her opening. She tasted good and I enjoyed her juices as they coat my tongue.

"Yes baby. Oh. Mmm yes," she moaned as she raised her legs and hips, pulling me deeper into her. I stuck my tongue inside her as deep as I could go and flex it from narrow to thick as she grinded against my face, fucking herself.

I pulled my tongue out of her and lapped at her clit.

"Oh. Yes. Right there," she moaned as her body bucked against my face. I fought her pearl, winning with every blow until I captured it and sucked on it as my tongue beat her down relentlessly. She panted as she squeezed her thighs, trapping my head between her legs as they trembled from her orgasm.

I loved when she orgasmed like this. I kept opening her legs, wanting to taste her juices. I continued to lap away at her pussy, trying to drink all she could give me until I feel she had enough.

I stood up to get undressed and as I took off my shirt, I instructed Erin to play with her pussy for me. I continued to watch her work two fingers into her fat wet folds until I was completely naked. I was about to give her something that would keep her happy for the rest of the day. I climbed on top of her and let my member rest against her warmth.

"You want this?" I asked, staring at her as I grabbed her neck and kissed her.

"No baby, I need it," she panted reaching down and placing me at her opening. As I press forward causing her to gasp for air, I stroke deep, burying myself into her. She was all mine for the taken.

Renee

I was sitting out front of my house in my car having a mental breakdown. I felt so overwhelmed by everything that I couldn't stop my tears from falling. I don't know whether it was my pregnancy hormones or just that reality was setting in. It seemed like my life was a mess and I didn't know where to begin to get it back together.

I didn't even really want to go in the house after seeing Christopher's car still parked in the driveway. I knew my presence could lead to many questions, telling him the news of getting fired and being pregnant was surely going to stress him out.

I had to use the bathroom, so I grabbed my purse and headed inside. I opened the door and luckily Christopher was nowhere to be found, and I was hoping like hell he was upstairs sleeping. I had time to get myself together and prepare myself for the conversation I knew was to come. I dropped my purse on the sofa, headed straight towards the downstairs bathroom, and when I finished, I sat there for a while thinking since I was home for the day I might as well go ahead and start preparing for dinner.

After figuring out how to start the dreaded conversation, I figured I would get out my scrubs and into some house clothes. I headed upstairs towards my bedroom when I heard something that stopped me in my tracks.

"Mmm… yes!" My stomach immediately felt queasy. I was hoping this wasn't what I thought it was. I headed towards our back room—the room Christopher was staying in, and as I walked down our hallway, I heard it again.

"Yes, yessss, right there," a woman moaned, and I heard what sounded like flesh smacking against each other. I peeked into the room and got the shock of my life. Not only was my husband cheating but with a white bitch at that. She was on top of him with her head thrown back humping against what I knew was bringing her sexual bliss.

"Shit. I'm coming Chris. Oh fuck, yess, yess, yessss," She groans bucking like a wild woman. I knew that voice…

I couldn't stop myself as I walked in the bedroom. "You trifling bitch!" I screamed as I leaped on the bed.

"I can't fucking believe you, you backstabbing bitch!" I swung wildly at her face as we fell off the bed and crashed on the floor with her landing first. "This is what you've been trying to do?!" I struck her and she managed to kick me from off her. I regained my balance and tried to charge ass, but Chris stepped in the way with his naked self, trying to intervene. I swung on him too, striking him square in his face, making him almost fall on top of Erin. He managed to keep his footing and that frustrated me even more as I hit him with a series of blows.

"You dirty dick nigga!" I screamed, only for him to eventually grab my wrists. "Get the fuck off of me!"

I kicked him in his groin and when his grip loosened, I took advantage of that opportunity to get at Erin as she got to her feet.

"I'm not finished with you bitch! You slut! You supposed to be my fucking best friend!" I shouted as I grabbed a handful of her hair and struck her across the jaw. She swung back and Chris grabbed me from behind trying to pull me off her but I had a great grip on her hair at that point.

"Let her hair go, Renee!" Christopher screamed.

"Shut the fuck up pussy!" I screamed at him as I turn my attention on him. "You trifling dirty dick nigga. How long you been fucking this bitch?" I asked, letting go of Erin's hair. I tried to elbow him, but it was useless. I couldn't get out of his hold if I tried.

"Get dressed Erin, damn!" Christopher shouted as Erin scurried around the room to get her clothes.

"I'm going to kill you, you shiesty bitch!" I screamed trying to wiggle out of his hold as she exited the room. When she was gone, Chris let me go and I turned to swing on him again, but this time he grabbed me up and pinned me to the wall.

"Stop fucking hitting me, Renee!" He screamed in my face and I spit in his.

"Fuck you, pussy!" I said. I wished I was a man to beat his ass and before I knew it Chris smacked me so hard, I didn't even know I fell to the floor.

"I told you about the disrespectful shit, Renee," he said to me while he was standing over me.

"Pussy! You're a bitch!" I still managed to say as I left the room to go downstairs and retrieve my purse. I grabbed my phone and hit the emergency call button to call the cops.

"Hello 911. What's your emergency?" The female dispatcher said on the other end of the phone.

"I need the police. I just got assaulted by my husband," I told her as I was looking at him dead in his eyes.

"What's your name and address?" the lady asked.

"My name is Renee Collins, and I live at 357 Meeting House Road. Please hurry, he's still here," I said into the phone as he made his way downstairs.

"I got the police on the phone, pussy. You are going to jail for putting your hands on me!" I stated.

"Whatever." Christopher said, heading out the door. I ran to the window and watched as he got inside his car. All I heard is, "Mrs. Collins, are you okay, Mrs. Collins?"

"Yes, I'm alright. Please, just hurry," I said before disconnecting the call.

I couldn't believe this shit. I took a seat on the sofa and cried my fucking eyes out. I wasn't perfect, but I didn't deserve this type of betrayal. I couldn't believe those two hurt me like that.

I noticed an open envelope on my table and picked it up, along with the letter and began to read it.

"Zya Collins?" I said, not believing what I was reading. "I'm going to kill that bitch!" I screamed loudly enough for the neighborhood to hear.

NEEDING HELP
Kelly

It had been four days, and I haven't heard from Adrian since we came back from Laguna Beach. I thought was a dream come true, but it seemed to be slowly turning into a nightmare. I called and left plenty of messages, but I got no response from him. I just hoped Adrian was okay. He had me thinking that opening up and telling him how I felt about him was a mistake. I believe I scared him away and the mention of me having or developing deeper feelings for him just wasn't what he had in mind.

"Come on Kelly, stop dwelling on it so much. He's probably just busy and has something important to take care of," Sophia said, trying to snap me out of my funk, as she took a seat across from me. We were at her house sitting in her dining room talking about my problems.

"I'm not thinking or worried about Adrian, Sophia. I told you, I'm just enjoying the company and myself for the moment," I said, lying through my teeth. Truth be told, I was heartbroken and rejected. I just couldn't admit it.

"I hear what your mouth is saying Kelly but-" she paused to take a sip of her drink before she continued. "The look you have in your eyes when you speak of him tells a different story. I've known you for years and I see a totally different Kelly," she says looking at me.

That was the thing about Sophia; she paid attention to entirely too much. I kept my mouth shut, hoping she would let the conversation die.

"So, you're just going to ignore me, Kelly?" Sophia asked.

"I'm not ignoring you, Sophia." I really was.

"So, tell me the truth then. You're my girl, Kelly and you know I can read you. So, what's up? Are you falling for this guy or something?" I looked at her wishing she'd just drop the subject, but she didn't. "Oh my god Kelly! You are, aren't you?" She took another sip of her wine and said, "He gave you some of that dark meat and you lost it. Jesus Christ, I thought you were able to handle casual sex."

"Sophia!" I shouted, throwing the half-eaten milky way candy bar at her.

"What? I'm just saying."

"You need to put a filter over your mouth, that's what. And for your information, it's not just the sex. I mean, the sex is phenomenal, but it's not just that. He's actually a great guy to be around. He makes me feel so special and alive at moments. It's kind of hard to explain honestly," I told her. If it were her, she'd get addicted too.

"It's okay, Stella. Just as long as you get your groove back. I mean there's no need to try to explain it. I know or at least can imagine the feeling," she said, showing her wedding band and engagement ring. "I just hope you're being careful. I don't want to see you hurt in any." Right then, her husband, Dave, came walking down the steps and into the kitchen to grab something to snack, and Sophia and I just sat there quietly watching him.

Dave was a good guy. He was sure about himself and what he wanted in life, had a nice, toned body and a nice tan and all he did was live to love Sophia. As I sat there in silence, that was when I realized that was what I wanted too. That was the kind of love I want to be smitten with.

"Why y'all two so quiet?" Dave asked, appearing from the kitchen and looking at the two of us skeptically. We looked at each other before looking back at him and said, "No reason."

"Right, Y'all probably talking about chick stuff, but okay I get it. I'm out of here." He headed up the stairs back to where he came from as me and Sophia shared a laugh. When Dave was out of ear shot and the coast was clear, we started talking again.

"I know what you mean Sophia, but truth be told I'm really falling for this guy. Adrian just feels like everything I've been waiting for, but I think he has commitment issues. Ever since we were back home, I got nothing. No phone calls or messages. Not even an email," I said, slumping in my chair.

"Wow...talk about disappointment. That sounds bad, like a one-night stand that lasted too long. Did you use protection?" she asked, and I gave her a look that indicated hell no. "Kelly, come on! You know better. How many times did y'all do the deed?"

"Sophia! I'm telling you about how I feel rejected and disappointed, and you go straight to the sex," I snapped on her.

"Sorry, I just want to make sure we have our bases covered. Men are dogs," she said.

"Too many to count," I answered honestly as Sophia shook her head at me.

"Wow, you're a little slut," Sophia said, starting to laugh.

"It's been years and I've been deprived. I got caught up, don't judge me," I said.

"Hell, you know I'm not, but I'm just saying what if you ended up pregnant and now, he's M.I.A... did he at least pull out?" she asked as I shook my head no. I felt like I was being chastised by my mother. "Did you use a plan B?" I shook my head no again. "Yeah, you trippin', girl. You would risk your life like that. You can't trust these men out here."

"Says the married friend," I countered.

"That doesn't mean anything; I just held on to a good one," she retorted. I mean that was true, but that's why I tried my best to get something like her. she had what every girl wanted–happy marriage.

But I was over here going through my own problems. How could I tell her I was pregnant without her giving me a speech on my life. I just wanted her to be happy for me, but after our little girl talk, who knew how she was going to feel.

Fuck it, I thought. "Sophia, I'm pregnant!"

"Un-fucking-believable," she managed to say.

"I know, I know." I put my head down thinking about my situation.

"So, what are you thinking? Do you even know where he lives because we can stalk his ass," she said pulling out her phone. There was just a lot to process all at once, especially with Adrian all of a sudden fallen off the face of the earth.

"I went to one of his houses before, but I don't believe he stayed there much. He's a real estate agent and he owns many homes." I teared up thinking about his antics, and Sophia rushed over to my side.

"It's okay Kelly. It's okay. I'm going to be here for you from start to finish, I promise. If having this baby is what you plan on doing, then I'll support you every step of the way. But we still got to get in contact with him somehow. Just know that you are not alone," Sophia said, holding me and rubbing my shoulder. I was grateful for her comfort. I needed it right now and I needed a good friend.

"Thanks Sophia." I managed to say as she just kept rocking me.

Adrian

I had just arrived at Set It Off to meet with Christopher and Matthew so we could handle a few things and to also break the news to Matt about our decision to change some things. Chris and I didn't feel as though it was a good idea to have him continue to play a part in our extracurricular business venture after the stunt our last visit to the club. It was careless and he seemed to have a problem staying focused especially when it came to women. I read a lot about great empires falling because of a woman, and I didn't want to be placed on that list with the rest of them.

I didn't want him to feel slighted though because he had been doing a great job running the club, so we decided to keep it to just that before he started pillow talking about other things that we got into.

"You ready to go inside?" Christopher asked. I nodded. We were sitting in my car and after finishing our conversation, I was stuck in my thoughts. Things made better sense to do them this way at least I thought so.

As we exited the car and walked towards the building, I couldn't help but to wonder what had happened to Chris' face, but I figured I would ask about it later. The scratches and swelling were evident, but I figured staying focused was more important now.

Cousin or no cousin business was simply that–business. It wasn't opening time, but a few girls had arrived early and were getting prepared as we spotted Amour at the bar when we entered.

"What's up Amour? Where is your boyfriend at?" Christopher asked, taunting her as he leaned over the counter. I took a seat on the stool. She rolled her eyes at Chris and turned her attention towards me.

"Hey Adrian," she said to me, ignoring him.

"What's up Amour?" I said not really caring for these two antics. I didn't understand why people complicated things. Business, sex, and romance didn't mix.

"Nothing at the moment. Y'all two just missed Matt by like ten minutes. He didn't say where he was going," she told us. Chris and I glanced at each other. That is what I meant about the way he did business. Matthew was a headache.

"Get him on the phone, Chris," I said to him. I watched him pull out his cellphone and call his stupid ass cousin.

"No answer Ad... This is some bullshit," Christopher stated while taking a seat now at the bar with me.

"Let's just wait awhile and give him a chance to get back."

"If he wasn't your cousin...man. He knew we were on our way. This is bad for business, Chris and you know how I am." I made my frustration known.

"Just calm down. I already know what you're thinking and it's bad, but don't let it get to you," Christopher said, trying to deescalate the situation.

"Get to me, huh? It looks like something already got to you. What happened to your face?" I asked, staring at Amour as she bent over to get something off the shelf under the register.

He took a deep breath and sigh before answering, "Renee happened to me."

"Renee! What the hell do you do for Renee to hurt you like that?" I asked him. I gave him my undivided attention and that caused him to lower his gaze, embarrassed.

"I got busted with Erin earlier today," Christopher admitted, which left me flabbergasted. I couldn't believe it, but I knew it was a matter of time before that affair hit the fan.

"What the fuck, Chris. I knew that was going to happen, man. I told you," I said to him while looking around to check and make sure we still had our privacy to speak openly. "What happened?"

"A long story, but it ended with Renee coming through like a tornado. She caught us smack dead in the middle of the act and if you think my face is bad you should imagine Erin's. Renee was all over her like a wild dog," he informed me.

"So where is Erin now? Is she okay?" I asked.

"Last we spoke, she was at the hospital." I shook my head at the thought of her injuries.

"I'm glad I don't have kids or a baby mama," I admitted.

"Keep it that way Adrian, it's stressful. I also think Renee called the cops on me," he told me.

"Why would she do that? Adultery and infidelity are not a crime," I told him.

"Things got physical Adrian."

"I can see that." I quipped.

"I mean from both sides," he says.

"Please don't tell me you put your hands on your wife," I said looking at him not believing what I was hearing. When Christopher remained quiet, I said, "The hell is wrong with you dude?! She's your wife!"

"Honestly, Adrian. I lost it, man." He rested his elbows on the bar with his head between his arms and fingers interlock around his neck behind his head. "I did...I mean, it happened out of instinct after she spit in my face. You know I love Renee, but it just happened," he explained. I sat there wondering why people got married. It was reasons like this that made me never want to get married. People commit to something they never will fulfill. I mean, sure it was not all glitz and glamour, but that was a fight you swore to your partner that you would fight with them.

If what you feel doesn't run that deep, then why say or even dedicate your life to another? I love sex like any other human being especially like any other man on this Earth, but a vagina and penis were only as good as the person they were connected to. I knew some men and women who made themselves orgasm strong enough to make their own toes curls and eyelids go heavy with just their own hands.

"Enough about my troubles though. You've been quiet since you were back what about your trip. How was it?" Christopher asked, changing the subject.

"It was a good vacation, I can say that much," I said, thinking about Kelly. I could see myself with her but I was too afraid to move to the next level. I was really starting to like her.

"How's Kelly? Did she enjoy herself?" he asked. I felt like a jerk for ignoring her, but I couldn't face her and continue to hold on to my principles that got me so far in life. I mean, look at where the emotional drama got Chris.

"Honestly I haven't spoken to her since returning from the trip," I admitted.

"Come on, Adrian. I thought you said she was different? What did she do wrong to get on the block list?" he asked looking over to me.

"She didn't do anything wrong. She actually did everything right, but I'm not trying to be in a committed relationship, and I can see where that was going." Looking at Chris' fucked up life, I realized I was good from where I was at.

"Well, your life is better than mine right now. Anyway, let's just get out of here and we'll just come back a little later. I don't want to just sit around here waiting for Matt," I said getting ready to leave.

"Y'all leaving?" Amour asked me to wipe the bar where we were seated.

"Yeah, but we'll be back. Just tell Matthew to call us when he gets back," I stated.

"Come on, Chris. I'm just going to ride with you. We'll be back anyway, plus I got to keep you sane. Those women are going to have you going crazy too," I said as we exited the front door and headed towards his car.

I had Kelly on my mind now. I missed her, and I just didn't want to admit it but I actually started to think that I was falling for her too.

OVER AND DONE
Erin

Here I was sitting in the back seat of a car getting driven from Einstein Hospital. My left eye was completely shut and was the size of a cherry tomato. I just finished getting x-rays to make sure I didn't have a broken orbital bone.

I couldn't believe I let Renee do that to me. That bitch had my blood boiling and I owed her an ass whipping for this shit. *She was lucky she caught me in the middle of an orgasm or things would've gone differently, but she got this one*, I thought to myself as I sat in the back of my Uber waiting to pull up. The doctor gave me some medicine to take the pain away, but I still felt the pain throbbing from my eye, and it was giving me a headache.

As the driver pulled up in front of my door, I noticed some brown-skinned dude leaving Christopher and Renee's driveway. I couldn't make out who he was, but my attention was shifted when I saw Renee at her front door. I was hesitant to get out at first, but I had to get a hold of myself and wondered when I ever let another woman intimidate me.

"Thanks, and have a good day," I said to the driver before opening my door. I kept my eye open on Renee and when she spotted me, she stepped out of her door and looked right at me as I tried to hurry up and make it to my house. I was no fool. I already had my house key in my and was grateful when I reached my front step.

"Don't try to run now, you trifling bitch!" Renee shouted as I inserted my key in the door. I might have wanted a piece of Renee, but I knew when to pick my battles and right now, with my eye, was not the time. I finally got my door unlocked and right before I shut it, I saw Renee coming up my front steps with a crazed look in her eyes.

Boom. Boom. Boom. She pounded on my door.

"Open the fucking door, Erin, you backstabbing bitch! You want to fuck my husband!" she shouted as she kicked my front door.

"Renee, please just go home! You're making a scene!" I screamed from my side of the door. Knowing our nosy ass neighbors, they were going to be at their doors and hanging out their windows at sound of the commotion.

"Scene!? BITCH! You were supposed to be my best friend and I caught you sleeping with my husband! My fucking husband, bitch! I don't give a fuck about these people! Come out the damn house, you white bitch! Don't be scared now!" she hollered for all to hear.

I put my back against the door. I couldn't believe this; this was embarrassing and I wished I was in the right health to open this door and give her everything she was looking for in front of all the onlookers out there.

"Oh, and here, bitch" Renee shouted and a few seconds later a brick came in and crashed through my front window.

I grabbed it and saw a piece of paper on it. When I opened it, I realized exactly what it was. The DNA results are about Zya.

"No matter when or where I see you, I'm going to beat your ass, Erin. I swear on everything, bitch! Watch your fucking back!" Renee declared. I sat on the floor, thinking about this whole ordeal.

Yes, I knew what I was doing and did I regret it but.. *Hell no! I love that man and as soon as I get healed up and this swelling goes down I'm going to beat her ass for that window!* I thought as I picked myself up off the floor and grabbed my phone and try to call Christopher to tell him what just happened. I also wanted to tell him to pick up Zya from school because I couldn't drive in my condition, but I received no answer from him. I wondered what the hell he could be doing at this time. I mean, I just got finished texting him before I left the hospital.

I was growing more frustrated, and my head started to pound more as I settled on calling my sister and asking her if she could pick up her favorite and only niece.

"Hello?"

"Hey Michelle, I need a favor please. It's important," I inform her, trying to soften her up. "I need you to pick Zya up from school for me. I can't drive at the moment."

"Oh my God, and what's wrong with you Erin?" Michelle asked me like I was interrupting her busy day, which I knew I wasn't. My little sister didn't do a damn thing for a living but live off our parents who spoiled her young ass because she was their baby.

"My eye is swollen shut. Now can you pick up Zya or not?" I asked, irritated. "Listen, it's a long story Michelle, but when you get here, I'll tell you everything," I said before disconnecting the call and grabbing the broom out of the closet to clean up the glass off my living room floor. Renee had every right to feel whatever she was feeling, but I was still planning to kick her ass, and I didn't give a fuck if I was wrong.

I went back to the kitchen to retrieve some ice out of the freezer to put on my face. That shit stung but I knew it was needed to get the swelling down. I took a seat on my sofa and tried to find me something to watch and kicked my shoes off to get more comfortable. Soon enough, just as I started watching a movie on TV, the TV started watching me, and I doze off.

Christopher

I figured I would go to my mom's house to ask her if she would keep Siren for a few days or a week while Renee and I settled our differences at home. I didn't want Siren around our negativity or seeing me and her mom arguing or fighting. I just hoped my mother wouldn't assault me next after I told her what went down earlier.

Evangeline was very strict on marital values, so to tell her about all the infidelity in my marriage along with her having another granddaughter was going to be a lot to take in. So many thoughts ran in my mind as Adrian and I drove to Abington, Pennsylvania. The car is quiet; I knew he was upset about Matthew's lack of business etiquette. Shit I was too, but I thought it was best to leave that subject alone.

"What's up Adrian? What's on your mind, buddy?"

"Besides business?" he asked me. "Thinking about Kelly and wondering if I'm playing this all wrong."

"I knew it, I knew it, I knew it. You've fallen for this woman. I knew it. I could tell; you never took no woman with you to California, ever."

"I didn't say all that. I just said I was questioning a few things on my part that's it," he said trying to clear up his spill.

"Yeah, all that sounds fine and all, but we can be honest with one another Adrian. We've been friends for years now. I can tell you, you're into her dude. You know, you never said one bad thing about this woman."

"It's nothing bad to say about her, yet," he answered.

"That's my point exactly. She's your dream girl." I stated.

"Nonsense. You know me and how I am Christopher-"

I cut him off. "Listen, and I don't mean any disrespect when I say this, but every woman out here is not your mom or one of your aunts who sneaks around or does a man dirty when they get a chance. You really need to grow out of that before you let a great woman pass you by."

"I can't help my comfort zone and what I grew accustomed to. That's just what I am seeing in my reality," Adrian started and as he talked, I noticed red and blue flashing lights in my rearview mirrors.

"I think the cops are pulling us over," I informed Adrian, which caused him to look back over his shoulder.

"It's alright, we're good right?" he asked.

"Yeah, we didn't get anything from the bar so we're clean," I told him as I pulled over to the side of the road. "Was I speeding?" I asked as Adrian shrugged. A moment late, the police officer tapped on my driver's side window.

I rolled my window down and asked, "Can I help you officer?"

"License, registration and proof of insurance please," One officer stated as his partner walked to the passenger's side of my car to keep a steady eye on Adrian. I reached for my papers which I kept in my glove compartment and when I did, I noticed the officers clutch at their pistols on their hips.

"I'm just getting the documents you asked for. Please, relax," I told them not wanting this to end with Adrian and I being left as a pair of dead black men over a misunderstanding. I handed over the information to the officer, and with one glance at my ID, he stated, "Mr. Collins I need you to exit the vehicle please."

"What? What for?" I wanted some answers.

"Please don't make me ask you again. Now." He actually opened my door and with one hand on his gun, he took a step back and repeated himself more hostilely. "Get the hell out the car." Soon, another patrol car arrived on the scene. I slowly exited the driver's side with my hands held high in the air.

"What's going on officer?" I was confused as to what this is all about.

"Turn around and place your hands on the vehicle," the taller officer commanded as the other officer that just arrived approached. I did as he said. He patted me down and grabbed one hand, placing it behind my back as he slipped a pair of handcuffs on my wrist.

"What am I being arrested for?" I asked.

"For assault on a Mrs. Renee Collins," the officer informed me.

"This is a big misunderstanding. My wife-" I tried to explain.

"I understand," he said, placing the other cuff on my other wrist. "Do you have any weapons on you or anything that can be used to harm you or myself?"

"No. You just patted me down," I answered.

"Now we are going to search your vehicle for any weapons. Is that okay with you?" He asked me like I had a choice. I just wanted them to search my shit so we could get this bullshit charge over and done with. I couldn't believe Renee really pressed charges on me when she was the one throwing hands.

"Whatever," I said frustrated as hell.

"Okay, we're going to need you to step out the vehicle also, sir." The shorter officer said to Adrian. Adrian just looked at me and then exited the car. They didn't handcuff him; they had him standing off to the side of the road as the two officers conducted their search of the car and the officer who arrived later on waited with Adrian.

Shortly after the officers came over to Adrian and told him to place his hands behind his back.

"Why? What did I do?" Adrian demanded.

"You have the right to remain silent. Anything you say or do can be used against you in a court of law-"

"What am I being arrested for?" Adrian shouted.

"You have a right to an attorney. If you can't afford one, one will be provided to you," the taller of the two officers said.

The shorter officer said, "Not sure of what kind of drugs, but for sure you are being charged with possession of a controlled substance," the officer said to the other who retrieved the duffle bag that was under my back seat that I totally forgot about.

"We want our lawyers!" I shouted. I couldn't believe I forgot about that. "Damn!" was all I could say. Today was filled with so much drama, I forgot about that part of business.

GIVE AND TAKE
Renee

"I understand," I said into the phone. I was just informed by a detective that Christopher was taken into custody earlier today.

"Are you sure you plan on pursuing this?" the detective asked me.

"Yes, I'm sure. I want that man in jail for putting his hands on me." I was tired of all these questions from these people. They already took a dozen pictures of my bedroom, my face, and the bruises over my body earlier, like what more did these people want from me?

"Okay, well that will be all Mrs. Collins, but I should also inform you that your husband is in deeper trouble than just this matter," the detective told me, which threw me for a loop.

"What does that mean?" I inquired, taking a seat at my dining room table.

"Well, I can't go into details but earlier when your husband was stopped by fellow officers, he and another party were in possession of some major drugs. Do you by any chance happen to know anything about that?"

"No. Why would I?" I answered as I think good fucking riddance. Serve his cheating ass right for sleeping with Erin's shiesty ass.

"Well, you never know now a days, but that will be all Mrs. Collins. If anything changes, and you have any new news or need any answers, please feel free to call me at my office number I left to you earlier. Thank you and have a good evening," he said just before disconnecting the call.

A part of me was concerned for Christopher but the spitefulness in me believed he deserved everything he was getting for betraying me the way he did. They had been sleeping with each other for years now if Zya was his daughter. How could I not see that? How could I be such a fool to let this happen and especially under my own roof. I questioned myself as my eyes got misty and I felt myself about to break down.

I figured I would go upstairs and check on Siren before I got in the shower and try to get some sleep. My body felt exhausted, but my mind had a million and one things running through it. I headed upstairs, and as I got almost to the top, there was a knock at my front door. Who could this be at nine at night?

As I walked back down the stairs I asked, "Who is it?" with more attitude than I meant to display.

"It's me ReRe," A male voice sounded behind the door.

"Who the hell is me?" I was irritated and wanting a name.

"Matt! Now come on, open the door," he said and I did. Matthew was just over earlier after I had just spoken to the cops. I called him to pick up Siren from school and thankfully, he came through for me.

"What's up Matt?" I asked stepping to the side to let him in the house.

"Did you hear anything from your husband? He was supposed to meet up with me today, but he never did. Someone at the bar said I missed him, so I was calling his phone, but it kept going to his voicemail."

"Well, he's in jail where he belongs," I stated proudly.

"Come on Renee, I told you that was not the way to go about that."

"Fuck Christopher! He shouldn't have put his hands on me like I was some dude on the fucking street!" I snapped. I was irritated at him telling me what I shouldn't do. He probably knew he was fucking that white bitch behind my back. Men do things like that–know something is not right and don't speak on it.

"I understand that, but calm down, Renee. I'm on y'all side, but another black man in jail not the answer," he explained to me.

"Matthew, your cousin had a baby with my best friend. My fucking best friend, out of all people and she's about Siren age. How am I supposed to feel?" I said and I can't fight my pain and anger any longer. I tried to fight back the tears but can't. "It's not just that Matt. I'm pregnant and now I'm left by myself with no husband. Oh and I can't forget I also have no job because I got fired from Jefferson Hospital earlier today." Matthew placed his arms around me to console me.

"Come on ReRe. Have a seat and calm down," he said guiding me to the sofa. "I didn't know it was this deep. Damn, y'all had a lot going on, but you don't need to be stressing though, Renee. I know it's a lot, but your family needs you to keep calm, especially if you plan on having a healthy baby. Christopher needs you. You're his wife. People make mistakes, and this is coming from me," Matthew said trying to lighten up the mood as he rubbed my shoulder and held me close. It felt so comforting.

"Make sure you drop the charges on him. He needs to be home with y'all to fix his problems." Then it dawned on me.

"It's not just me though, Matt. When I was talking to the detective less than an hour ago, he stated something about him and somebody else getting caught with some drugs or something, but they wouldn't go into any details with me," I explained.

"Damn that must have been Adrian. They both stopped past Set It Off earlier looking for me, but that's around the time I went to go get Siren for you," Matthew said resting his chin on top of my head. "Damn, if that's the case, they might be in some serious shit." Matthew leaned back and took out his cellphone.

"Thanks for being here for me though, Matthew. I really needed someone to lean on right now. I can't say for sure, but I'll at least think about dropping the charges against Christopher, but if what the detective says is true, I don't know much good that will do. I feel like my life is ruined right now," I admitted.

"Well let's just work on trying to fix it. How does that sound?"

"Sounds easier said than done," I started wiping my eyes and face.

"We're family. It's what we're for," Matthew said, getting up. "Now, let me go and tell my Aunt Eva what just went down. You know she's going to go crazy. I hope she can bear the news."

"Thanks Matt."

"No sweat," he said before exiting out the front door.

Adrian

I couldn't believe this. Here I was sitting in this filthy cell and everything about this place just disgusted me. They had me in these red scrubs which appeared to be worn previously, and they fed me next to nothing on these plastic trays. I just kept thinking back to how I allowed myself to be placed here, and every conclusion I could think of ended with a woman being the cause.

I thought and believed if Chris could have controlled his hormones and kept his penis in his pants or even in his own wife, he wouldn't have moved so reckless as to forgetting he already had the product stashed in the car. It wasn't even just that—he wouldn't have even had a warrant out for his arrest if it wasn't for him getting caught having sex with Erin in the very own home he shared with his wife. Pussy had him that blind that he moved that carelessly.

"Fuck!" I shouted, thinking about my current situation. I couldn't believe my downfall was over some pussy. I even included myself when I thought about it because if I didn't have Kelly on my mind, I would've thought better than to get in that car with Chris after he just told me he wasn't sure if Renee called the cops on him or not.

I made a foolish decision, but I was out of there as soon as my bail hearing took place. When I spoke to my attorney, Anita Seth, she informed me that the only hold up in my release was that the courts just needed to verify where the money came from. In order for it to be accepted by the court due to the severity of the number of drugs that I was so called in my possession.

She also informed me that she didn't think it would be a problem was due to my profession as a realtor. They were holding me on a million-dollar bail and Chris was being held on the same, but I didn't have time to worry or focus on another man when I had more than enough on my plate. I figured as long as I was out there it will be a bit easier on the both of us.

I needed to be out there–I could at least help him after I got out, especially with my resources. On another note, I couldn't wait to tell Chris about himself. I mean, what man in their right mind forgets they had a car full of drugs that could possibly send you to prison for the rest of your life? It was so idiotic.

This was some complete bullshit, but I was just happy Chris wasn't a damn snitch. I had enough of staring out my cell door at these other inmates. I laid down in my bunk; my thin ass mattress was far from comfortable, but it was where I would rather be than talking and interacting with some of those guys. I wasn't looking down on them or anything, I just didn't plan on being here for too much longer.

I had two more days until my hearing and when that day came, I expected my freedom, at least for a brief moment while this case played out. If that wasn't bad enough, I also found out my hearing would be held in front of what I learned would be Judge Kelly Patten, herself.

I had wishful thinking, but she was no fool; I'm sure me ignoring her calls and emails didn't go over well with her. When I discovered who would preside over my case, my heart dropped to my feet. I discussed my discomfort with my attorney, and she believed we should see how things turned out at the hearing and that we could always use me and her personal relationship as leverage or for later argument if she does not recuse herself.

I figured she knew what she was talking about, but to be honest, if it was my choice, I wouldn't want to face Kelly. Only time would tell.

COMING TO AN END
Erin

It was the day of Christopher's bail hearing and I made sure I was at Montgomery County Courthouse bright and early. My eye was still a bit swollen, but it went down a lot considering what it once, and now I was able to see out of it once again. I had some discoloration around it, but that was nothing a big pair of Chanel glasses couldn't hide.

"What courtroom is he supposed to be in, Erin?" Michelle asked me. My sister was there as my support and was also my driver until I felt comfortable enough to drive myself.

I didn't know if Renee would decide to show up and if she did, I wanted someone I knew I could trust to have my back to be there with me if shit went down. I knew I wasn't one hundred percent healed, but I was enough to try my hand if I saw an opportunity.

"They told me courtroom G and also that it's scheduled for nine in the morning," I informed her as we searched for the right direction and headed that way.

"That's funny. Courtroom G, for some G-shit because after what you told me, that's all this seem to be," Michelle said.

"What are you talking about Michelle?"

"I'm talking about your life. You have to admit, what you told me is crazy. Now look at you here, being a ride or die chick and a baby mama," she said. I can't believe she found this shit amusing. Shit, I was nervous as hell as if I was the one who committed the crime.

"You really get off on this don't you?" I stated, irritation becoming quite clear.

"No, I'm just saying."

"This is not a game, Michelle. Please I'm stressing the hell out behind this," I admitted.

"Just calm down. Everything will work itself out. You need to stop stressing yourself out. Oh my god, hold that thought. Guess who just walked in?" she said. My eyes follow her line of sight and as soon as I spotted Renee, my blood boiled and my heartbeat sped up.

This was honestly my first time seeing Renee since the day that bitch threw that brick through my front window. She was with the same brown-skinned dude that day.

"Bitch," I state under my breath as I stared at her. She stared back at me and walked past me. I gave her the stank look.

"Erin, you should calm down. This is not the place for a scene," Michelle told me.

"I am calm. What are you talking about?" I asked, still not taking my eyes off Renee.

"Well, why are you tapping your foot like that?" she asked and I look down not even realizing I was doing so. "I can understand you wanting to get at her, but inside of a courthouse where there are a bunch of cops is not the appropriate place for neither of you, and it for damn sure is not for Chris' sake." Why did she have to make all this sense in the world now? Regardless, my bruised ego was dying for a fair shot at Renee.

"You're right, but don't let me find out you're scared of this bitch or something," I stated disappointed that I had to be in her presence without being able to whoop her ass.

"You might be my big sister, but don't get slapped. I fear no bitch. I'm just not that stupid or dick crazy to be getting hauled off to jail." I could tell Renee was staring back to me, but I tried my best not to look in that bitch's direction again. "Who's the guy she is with? He's cute."

"I don't know, and I have never seen him before. He is probably her family or something, but how can you think he's cute? He's with the fucking enemy, Michelle. Now who's dick crazy with your thirsty ass?"

"See, I know you're in your feelings so I'm going to just let that slide," she said, looking at her watch. "It should be time for them to begin, what's the hold up?"

"Your guess is as good as mine," I said as a Sheriff walked into the courtroom guiding Christopher and his friend, Adrian, along with another Sheriff trailing them from the rear.

"Here we go, I guess," she said.

Christopher looked stressed out. I knew he was, and I could tell by how he sounded over the phone after just a few days in there that this was getting to him. Seeing him like that made me start to worry even more about the outcome of this mess. He said they found some drugs in the car, but he wouldn't go into any details about what exactly happened or what would likely happen to him. I believe that's what made me feel the way I was feeling now. Fear of the unknown…

"Are you okay, Erin? You're shaking?" Michelle asked, squeezing my hand.

"Just a bit nervous, but I'll get over it," I claimed.

"Alright, but just remember I'm here for you and with you." I was so grateful to have her here with me at that very moment.

"Thanks, Michelle. You really are coming through for me. This is why you are my favorite sister," I said.

"Erin, I'm your only sister," she corrected me.

"Same difference." I smiled to let her know I was alright. I was just ready to get this show on the road and get it over with. I just wished they would hurry up and start.

Kelly

I couldn't believe this at all. After trying to contact Adrian all this time, his name appeared on my desk as one of my cases that I would have to preside over. What a turn of events. The embarrassment and rejection I felt because of this man made me so angry, and yet I still felt so sympathetic towards him. I couldn't even really say it was just that. Could I really send my future child's father to prison? Could I really be a fair, impartial judge when I was so emotionally involved?

These were some of the questions I asked myself. My integrity was on the line and so was my heart.

"Shit!" I said out of frustration. I was in my chambers going back and forth with myself about this situation. I was scheduled to preside over Adrian's bail hearing that day and I knew I had to recuse myself and request a change of venue but having Adrian by the balls just seemed so empowering after the stunt he pulled on me.

I placed my hand over my lower abdomen as I thought about what the day would bring. He was the reason I was shedding tears at night. He didn't even know that life was growing inside of me. He didn't even know he was about to become a father.

Oh well, the law is the law and I had always been a firm believer of that fact. That's how I had been doing my job, so that's how I was going to continue to do so. On top of that, he shouldn't have even lied to me. He shouldn't have led me to believe he was anything more than a drug dealer.

I grabbed my black robe from off the hook and put it on. I was ready to get this show on the road.

Knock, knock, knock.

Megan appeared. "We are ready whenever you are."

"Okay thanks. I'm on my way," I stated as she closed the door behind her.

I checked the mirror I kept in my chambers to make sure I looked presentable. Who was I kidding? I was making sure I looked damn good for this proceeding and when I gave myself the once over and everything appeared to be to my liking, I exited my chambers and entered the courtroom.

"Stay focused out there, Kelly." I told myself as I opened the door. Ready or not, Adrian. Here I come.

ABOUT RAVEN SMITH

RAVEN SMITH is a Philadelphia native whose interest in writing stemmed from coming in 2nd place in a poetry contest in 2012. She knew in high school she wanted to follow a creative path and she Graduated from Saint Joseph University with a B.A. in Liberal Studies with a major in Professional Writing and English. She knew she had a story to tell, and *Who Would've Thought?* is the first of many.

www.ingramcontent.com/pod-product-compliance
Lightning Source LLC
Chambersburg PA
CBHW032015170626
46807CB00006B/2816